The Wife

Single Wide Female in Love
Book 4

By

Lillianna Blake

DEDICATION

To all women out there looking for love.
Don't forget to love yourself first. ☺

TABLE OF CONTENTS

CHAPTER 1

I jabbed at the keyboard with one pointing finger. After almost an hour spent in an attempt to get my latest book formatted correctly, I was ready to jab it with a hammer instead.

"Why?" I glared at the screen. "Do what you are supposed to do!"

"Shouldn't I be the one saying that?" Max leaned against the doorway of the bathroom and smiled at me.

I glanced over at him and took in the sight of his tanned skin. It stood out against his white and blue swim trunks.

"I'm sorry, Max—just five more minutes."

"You said that five minutes ago—and five minutes before that." Max folded his arms across his chest. "Sammy, have you forgotten that this is our honeymoon?"

"I'm so sorry—I haven't forgotten. I'm just trying to format this book so that I can launch the darn thing. If I could just get it to do what it's supposed to do." I sighed.

Max walked up behind me and rubbed his warm hands over the curve of my shoulders. No matter how furious I was at technology, I couldn't resist being relaxed by his touch. I sighed again and closed my eyes.

"We leave tomorrow for the next part of our honeymoon. I'm tempted to make sure your computer gets left behind."

"You wouldn't!"

"No, I wouldn't. I know how important your work is to you, but you have to remember our honeymoon is important too. Don't you think? I really thought you would like the surprise."

"Are you kidding? Bermuda has been amazing. There's nowhere else I'd have chosen. It's perfect. And there's still more? I have no idea where we're headed tomorrow but I'm sure it will be just as fantastic."

"But we're not done with Bermuda. We have a chance to go out for that last snorkeling class, but instead we're stuck here. Know what I mean?" Max frowned. "I'm not trying to be a nag here, but I want my time with you."

My heart warmed at his words. It meant so much to me that he wanted to spend time with me. What kind of message was I sending him by putting my work first?

"You're right. I'm sorry. Let me just change into my suit." I started to stand up, but he eased me back down into my chair.

"Hold on, this is important too. Show me what the problem is and maybe we can figure it out together."

"Really?" I smiled up at him. "I just can't get it to format correctly. Every time I try, it does half the document and not the other half. Then I try to do the other half and the first half changes back."

"Oh, that's simple." Max leaned over me and hit a few keys. Then he clicked the mouse.

Before my eyes, magic happened as everything lined up just the way it was supposed to.

"How did you do that? I've been fighting with this thing forever!"

"Were you watching?" Max chuckled.

I decided not to mention that I'd been too distracted by the scent of his skin and the heat of his closeness.

"All I know is that we make a great team, Max. Have you given any more thought to quitting your job and working with me?" I stood up and turned to face him.

Max glanced away toward the door of the suite.

"No more work talk, remember? I'm going to check and see if the class is still available. I'll meet you downstairs in the lobby."

Before I could protest he was out the door.

I frowned. I knew that he'd left so quickly to avoid the conversation.

The first few days of our honeymoon had been wonderful.

When we'd arrived in Bermuda, it was like I'd been

transported to a perfect magical place. I intended for the rest of our honeymoon to be just as great as that first day. There was no need to dwell on an issue that wasn't really an issue.

I sent off the book to my editor, then grabbed my swimsuit.

After wearing it a few times, I'd become comfortable in the bikini. Max adored me in it and requested that I wear it as much as possible. I had to oblige—it was a gift, after all.

The first day I'd stepped out on the beach had been a bit horrifying. My imperfect body in a bikini? Who wanted to see that?

It turned out that no one even batted an eye. The ground didn't open up and swallow me whole. In fact, after a few minutes of teeth clenching and tummy covering, I'd actually forgotten that I had the bikini on. All it took was Max splashing me with the warm crystal-blue water to make me forget about being insecure. Ever since then, I'd looked forward to putting on my bikini.

As I slipped into it, I glanced in the mirror. One of my concerns was that I would end up gaining weight on the honeymoon—with the pressure of the wedding off and the enjoyment of good food. However, Max and I spent almost all of our time in the water or in the bed, with lots of fresh healthy food in between. My body looked more toned than ever.

I smiled proudly at myself, then walked out to join

Max in the lobby. I didn't even bother to wrap the towel I carried around my body.

LILLIANNA BLAKE

CHAPTER 2

When I reached the lobby, Max turned to watch me walk down the last steps. He smiled as widely at me in that moment as he had the day of our wedding. It was easy to think of myself as the luckiest woman in the world with the way he looked at me.

I reached the bottom stop and he wrapped his arm around my waist.

"You look beautiful."

"Thanks." I kissed his cheek. "Did we make it in time for the class?"

"Just."

He led me to the back door of the hotel; it opened right onto the beach. A small group of people were gathered near the edge of the water.

"Alright, everyone, we're going to get started now that we're all here." The instructor gave me a look.

I pretended not to notice. He was young, slender, and very tan. His brown hair was tied at the back of his neck. I imagined him with a fish tail and a little coconut-shell bra. When I giggled Max looked over at me.

"What?" He raised an eyebrow.

I almost told him it was nothing, then I thought better of it. Max deserved to know some of the quirky thoughts that went through my mind. I leaned close and whispered the visual into his ear.

He covered his mouth with his hand and turned away from me. At first I thought he might be upset, then I saw his shoulders shake. He cleared his throat and turned back to look at me with a gleam in his eyes.

"Thanks, now I'm never going to get that picture out of my head."

"Excuse me. We are reviewing very important safety information." The instructor put his hands on his hips.

"Sorry." Max smiled.

I took his hand in mine. It was rather fun to get into trouble with Max.

Once we all understood the instructions and had the equipment fitted onto our bodies, the instructor led us into the water.

"Now the most important thing to remember when you're underwater is not to panic. No matter what you see, the best way is the calm way."

Those words made me a little nervous. What might I see that would make me panic?

Max winked at me from behind his mask. I reminded myself not to let paranoia creep into my mind.

As we waded into the water I focused on its warmth and color.

Under the water, a new world opened up before me. I never thought much about what hid beneath the waves. Now I was amazed that I'd never thought to look before.

The colorful fish, the coral, and the plant life all blended together to become one of the most beautiful scenes I'd ever witnessed.

Max brushed his hand lightly over mine. I smiled around the mouthpiece. Now I understood why he was so anxious to get into the last class. I never would have known what wonders I was missing.

A plume of sand, brushed up from the bottom of the sea by the instructor's flipper, blurred my vision for a moment. When it cleared, I caught sight of something unexpected. A smooth silvery surface drifted by only a few feet away from me. When I caught sight of the long tapered snout my heart pounded.

It couldn't be a shark, could it?

I was sure that the instructor wouldn't bring us out to an area where sharks would be. Then again, it was the open sea. What would stop a shark from swimming wherever it wanted to?

I grabbed Max's hand and started moving backward.

Max looked at me with narrowed eyes behind his mask. He must not have seen the shark. The instructor was further ahead with the rest of the group. Max and I fell further and further behind.

Max tugged at my hand in an attempt to swim after the instructor. I shook my head and pointed in the direction of what I'd witnessed.

Max again narrowed his eyes. He pointed up toward the surface of the water. I nodded. We both swam up toward the surface. If the instructor noticed, he didn't turn back.

Once I broke through into the sunlight, I pulled the mouthpiece away from my mouth and took in fresh air. Max broke the surface beside me and did the same.

"Sammy, what's wrong? Are you hurt? Are you sick?"

"No, I'm not hurt. I saw a shark!"

"A shark?" Max half-smiled. "Seriously?"

"Max! I'm serious! I saw a shark swim a few feet away from me!"

"There's no way you saw a shark. We're in shallow water. Sharks don't come this close to the shore."

"Max!" I stared at him. "Do you think I'm lying? Do you think I'm making up seeing a shark?" My voice rose. "I know a shark when I see a shark, and that was a shark! I can't exactly shout shark underwater!"

"Sammy! Keep your voice down!" Max pointed past me to the beach. All of the people that had been swimming or playing in the water ran out to the safety of the sand because of all my shouting about a shark.

"So? They should get out of the water and so should we! I'm telling you that I saw a shark! You can stay here and tell that shark to its face that it doesn't belong here, but me—I'm out of here." I turned and started to swim. When I didn't hear Max splashing behind me I looked over my shoulder. "Are you coming?"

He glanced back down at the water and then up at me. "I guess so. I still say it wasn't a shark."

He swam after me.

CHAPTER 3

I didn't feel secure until we were back on the beach. About that time the instructor surfaced and scanned the water. He waved to Max and me.

"What are you doing? I thought I'd lost you!"

I decided not to point out that he had.

"She thinks she saw a shark."

"Thinks? Thanks a lot for the support, Max." I shook my head.

"A shark?" The instructor laughed. "Where?"

"There!" I pointed to a flash of silver. "Right there, behind you! Shark!"

The people on the beach shrieked and ran further up the sand as if the shark might grow legs and crawl. The instructor spun around in the water. Then he shook his head.

"Do you mean Dolly?"

"Dolly?" I looked over at Max. "He's a mermaid, he named the shark."

"Sammy, sh!" Max tried not to laugh.

"Dolly is a dolphin that we rehabilitated. She's part of

our experience, and you would have had the opportunity to pet her. She is most certainly not a shark. Now what was the first rule?"

I gulped as I recalled the instruction not to panic. Apparently that rule had not stuck in my mind.

"Sorry." I winced and looked over at the terrified people on the beach. "My mistake. No shark—just a dolphin."

"A vicious, deadly, Sammy-chomping dolphin." Max wrapped his arms around me. "I'll protect you from that horrible beast."

"Ha ha." I frowned. "I'm sorry I ruined the whole experience."

"Are you kidding?" He kissed my forehead. "I've never swum for my life before. Now I can check it off my list."

"You're so sweet to me." I kissed him.

He held me close and our kiss deepened. It wasn't until I heard the splashing of swimmers getting back into the water that I remembered we had an audience.

"I guess we should get back in the water."

Max looked into my eyes. "Or we could get back into the honeymoon suite."

I grinned. "I like the way you think, Max."

"Well, you did just save me from a shark—there are ways I should repay you."

We both laughed as we walked back toward the hotel to turn in our equipment.

The next morning—very early—after we'd check out of our hotel, Max hailed a cab to drive us to our next destination. I had no idea where it was.

"Are you going to give me a hint?" I stuck out my bottom lip.

"No, no hints."

"Why not?"

Max patted my knee. "It's supposed to be a surprise."

"I thought being in Bermuda was the surprise."

"Oh, that's just the beginning, sweetheart. You've been talking so much about how you want to travel—how life should be an adventure—so that's what I thought I'd give you for our honeymoon." He smiled.

I smiled back at him. I wanted to believe that he had something wonderful in mind, but his words concerned me. Did he think that a whirlwind honeymoon—as amazing as it was—would be all that I needed for the rest of our lives? My chest tightened with dread at the thought of being pinned down to one place for too long. Part of my life plan had always been to have the freedom to roam.

"Don't worry, you're going to love it." Max moved his hand from my knee to take my hand.

I smiled at him through the flickering of the early morning darkness. He said, "It's a bit of a drive, you might want to take a nap."

I leaned my head against his shoulder and closed my eyes. The rock of the car, the warmth of his body, and my exhaustion from our active few days swept me right into a deep slumber.

I awoke to the jolt of the brakes. My eyes flew open. Max still held me in his arms.

"It's okay, we almost missed the turn."

"It's not an easy road to see." The driver looked in the rear-view mirror. "Sorry, miss."

"It's okay." I smiled, though I wondered just where we were headed. A glance at my phone showed me that it was close to dawn. "Max? Any hints now?"

"No need to give hints when we're so close."

"Fine." I pouted.

The cab wound its way up a curvy road. I didn't see the beach—only trees. Then we drove out of the trees into a wide-open clearing.

"Is it a picnic?"

"Not exactly."

The cab turned down a road with a sign that showed a helicopter on it. I thought that was strange, but I was sure it had nothing to do with where we were going. Then the cab pulled into a long driveway. At the end of it, there was a large hangar. Beside the large hangar was a small helicopter.

"Max?"

He grinned.

The cab pulled to a stop. Max hopped out and ran

around to the other side of the car to open my door for me.

I almost refused to get out. There was a lot I was willing to try. A helicopter had never been on any of my lists.

"Aren't you excited?" Max offered me his hand to help me out of the cab.

I took it and hoped he didn't feel the tremble in my grasp. I looked at the helicopter as he led me toward it.

"Uh, this is a surprise."

"Isn't it great?" Max smiled so wide that his eyes squeezed almost shut. I knew he was proud of himself.

"It's something." I cleared my throat and stared at the helicopter. "It's small, isn't it?"

"It's a helicopter, not a jet." Max laughed. "Ready to get on?"

"Uh, maybe in just a minute." I squeezed my hands tight together and then released them. "I think that we should talk about this."

"Talk about what?" He frowned. "I thought you would love this. You're always so daring. Wait until you see the view!"

"Max, I know how much effort you put into this surprise, but I just don't know if I can do this."

"Sammy, you flew on a plane to Bermuda." Max shook his head. "This is the same thing."

"No, actually, it's quite a bit different. A plane is big—and it has lots of seats—and you don't have to look out the window if you don't want to. This is not a plane at all. This is like a bubble—a bubble, Max."

"I can assure you—it's stronger than a bubble." He grinned. "Where's your sense of adventure?"

CHAPTER 4

My heart pounded against my chest. Max's bright smile and reddened cheeks made it clear that he was excited. Unfortunately, I did not feel the same way. In fact, I felt as if I might throw up before I could even get on the helicopter.

A man walked out of the hangar.

"Hello, folks, are you ready for your flight?"

"I think we might need a minute." Max frowned.

"A minute is about all you have. We have to fly out soon or we'll miss our window."

"Okay, just one minute." Max assured him. Then he turned back to me. "What do you say, Sammy, can you try this?"

"Max, really—I just don't think this is for me."

"Please?" He took my hand in his. "I promise, once you're up there, you're going to forget all about your fears."

I looked into his eyes. The last thing I wanted was to disappoint him. I took a deep breath and nodded.

"Alright. But don't blame me if I scream and cry the entire time."

"You're going to need these." The pilot handed Max a set of headphones.

"Well, that's quite rude!" I frowned. "Do you treat all women this way? Giving their husbands headphones to block them out?"

"Uh." The pilot looked from me to Max, and then back to me. "These are yours." He held another set of headphones out to me. "The chopper can get pretty loud."

I blushed and took the headphones. "Thanks."

"It might drown out some of the screaming though, right?" Max winked at me.

"Ugh."

Max hugged me tight. "It's going to be great, I promise."

I looked over at the helicopter. I tried really hard to believe him.

Max slid his headphones on and then helped me get mine straight. He smiled at me and leaned in for a kiss.

My heart fluttered—but for once, not out of passion. I wanted to be as excited as Max was, but I couldn't bring myself to overcome the fear that boiled within me.

Against my better judgment, I climbed into the helicopter. It was smaller than I'd expected. That didn't make me feel any better.

"Is there a weight limit on these things?" I frowned as

I settled into my seat.

Max sat down beside me and shot me a look. "Sammy, don't start with that nonsense." He laughed lightly.

The pilot checked to make sure that we were both strapped in. My stomach lurched when he took his position in front of the controls. The last chance for me to beg out of the helicopter stared me right in the face.

"Oh, Max, I don't know." I squeezed his hand tight.

"Trust me." Max smiled at me.

If he said more, I didn't hear it. The blades of the helicopter roared to life. I closed my eyes. I tried to remind myself of all of the amazing things that I'd accomplished—things I never thought I was capable of doing, yet they had been checked off my bucket list— which made me believe that this too could be checked off.

I felt the helicopter lift. My stomach seemed to rush up into my throat. Sweat gathered on my palms. In the back of my mind I knew that my grip on Max's hand might lead to physical injury.

Max snuggled closer to me. Over the roar of the helicopter he managed to get a few words through. "Open your eyes, Sammy!"

I didn't want to. I thought if I kept my eyes closed through the entire journey, I might be able to make it. But Max tugged at my hand until finally I opened my eyes. The sight before me took my breath away.

A beautiful sunrise painted across the sky, surrounded us. It was dotted with wisps of white puffy clouds. When I looked a little further I could see the lush green hills that we were flying over.

I looked over at Max. He smiled. Even though he didn't speak, I could hear him clearly say, "I told you so."

I looked back out the window. It was easy to see why Max had been so insistent. The bird's-eye view of the valley below filled my vision with blues, greens, oranges, whites, and the deep browns of the rich soil. My soul was nourished in a new way.

After a few minutes the helicopter swooped downward toward a landing pad. I braced myself. I'd survived the flight but would I survive the landing?

The helicopter rocked back and forth a little but made its way down to the landing pad without incident. When I opened my eyes, I saw that we were in the base of the valley. The chopper stilled.

Max helped me out of the helicopter. We handed over our headphones to the pilot. Max slid his arm around my waist and walked me to the edge of the landing pad.

"See? Wasn't it worth it?" He nuzzled the side of my neck.

I still felt the vibrations of the helicopter, but his arms around me eased my nerves.

"Yes, it was worth it. Thank you, Max. This is one adventure I never would have had on my own."

"That's the point, sweetheart. Now we get to start our adventure together. I want you to know that just because we got married, that doesn't mean the adventure stops. It's just the beginning."

"Oh, I love you, Max."

We shared a slow kiss.

It was so sensual that it seemed to stir the wind around us. My hair flew into my face. I curled up against Max as the wind whipped harder. I knew all of the commotion couldn't be created by us.

I turned to see the chopper had lifted up into the air.

LILLIANNA BLAKE

CHAPTER 5

"Wait, where is the helicopter going?" I grabbed Max's hand. "It's leaving us behind!"

"No, it's not, it's fine. We're going to hike out of the valley."

"Huh?" I looked up at the high hills around us. "What do you mean we're hiking out?"

"Don't worry, I have camp set up halfway up the trail so we can spend the night here. I thought you'd enjoy having the chance to make love under the stars." He smiled.

The thought was tempting, but the high hills were daunting.

"Do you really think we can hike all the way out? What if I can't make it?"

"I have no doubt that you can." Max looked into my eyes. "Don't doubt yourself now, gorgeous. We're a team, remember?"

"I appreciate your faith in me, Max, but I'm not so sure."

"Don't worry—if we run into any problems, I have a

way to contact the ranger and he'll send out a team to get us."

"Are you sure?

"I promise. This is going to be wonderful. You have to trust me, Sammy. I won't let anything happen to you. Don't you know that?" He looked into my eyes.

"I do." I smiled a little. "I guess this is just a bit more of an adventure than I was expecting."

"Don't worry, I have a map of the easiest trail and plenty of supplies waiting for us at the first stop." He held out his arm to me. "Ready to explore what the valley has to offer?"

"Yes. I'll explore anything with you by my side."

When we started to walk, I hid my concern. Sure, all of the activity I'd engaged in to get healthy had gotten me into better shape, but good enough shape for this much of a hike?

Max slid his hand into mine and pulled me up beside him.

"Together." He smiled. "We can get through anything."

His enthusiasm was infectious. The ground was even and the temperature was mild.

"I can't believe you planned all of this without ever telling me about it."

"This and much more." Max leaned into my arm and gave me a light nudge. "You're not the only one that can be creative, you know." He smiled over at me in a way that made me fall in love all over again as he continued speaking.

"You know, when I saw you walk down that aisle, I thought I had to be dreaming. The thing was, I didn't dare to pinch myself, because if it was a dream I never wanted to wake up."

"Wow."

"It's true."

"No. I mean wow, did that line ever work?" I grinned.

"Line?" He gasped. "Really, Sammy, the things that you think of me."

"It was sweet of you to say. I felt the same way looking at you, Max. In fact, sometimes I still wonder if this is all in my imagination…the amount of time I spent dreaming of even kissing you, and now we're married?"

"Oh, we have plenty of time on the hike for you to tell me all about those dreams and kisses." Max nudged me again.

"Never mind." I laughed. "I think that you get the point."

"We're almost to our first stop. Do you need a rest?"

"No, it's okay, I can make it."

Max nodded.

I was about to lean in for a quick kiss when I heard a strange rustling sound. It was not like any sound I'd ever heard before. It made my heart stop for a split second, though I wasn't sure why.

"What's that, Max?" I leaned closer to him.

"What's what?" He glanced over at me.

"You don't hear that sound?"

"What sound?"

"Sh. Listen." I stood still. The rustling sound came again.

Max's arm tightened around my shoulders.

"Don't move, Sammy."

"Huh? Why?"

"Just don't move."

"Max?"

"Sammy, can you promise me that you won't scream? You won't run?"

"Uh. I promise." I bit into my bottom lip. I wasn't sure that I could keep that promise.

"Okay, remember your promise, alright?" He locked his eyes to mine.

I nodded.

"There's a very large snake—only a few inches away from your right foot. Now, I can't tell what kind it is, but no matter what, we don't want you to get struck. So, take a deep breath. Sammy?"

I trembled as I continued to stare into his eyes. It took all of my willpower not to scream. I started to look in the direction of the snake.

"Don't. Don't look, Sammy." Max shook his head. "Seeing it is not going to make anything better. What I'm going to do is pick you up—very slowly."

"Max, you can't pick me up."

"Yes, I can. Don't argue with me. If I pick you up, then there's no way the snake can reach you."

"But what about you?"

"I'm far enough away that I should be able to dodge it if it strikes. Now on the count of three I'm going to pick you up. Don't fight me and don't scream."

"Okay." I tried not to think about whether he would be able to lift me. Max had picked me up before, but I still wondered if he could pick me up and hold me up.

"One, two, three!" Max swept one arm under the back of my legs and tipped my body back against him. In the same moment he lunged away from the edge of the path. He moved about three steps before he began to stagger.

"Max, put me down—you're going to get hurt!"

"No, I won't. Where's the snake?"

"It's gone. I don't see it."

"Oops!" Max wobbled back and forth. Then he sat down hard on the ground. I landed right in his lap.

"Did I hurt you?"

"I'm fine." He laughed. "I just lost my balance."

CHAPTER 6

As we continued along the path Max pointed out a few things along the way.

"Did you research this trip too?"

"Yes, I did. I wanted to make sure that I could impress you."

"You wanted to impress me?" I laughed. "That's silly."

"Why would that be silly?"

"Max, you don't have to do anything to impress me."

"I don't have to—I wanted to."

"But why? I adore you—no extra work needed."

Max raised an eyebrow. "It's good to know that you feel that way but I'm not so sure that you're right."

"What do you mean?"

"You're a writer. You're an adventurer. You're always thinking—about everything."

"I know, I know. It's a bad habit." I shook my head.

"No, it's an amazing habit, Sammy. Everything has meaning to you, everything matters. You see connections and inspiration in things. How are you not going to get bored with someone like me?"

I stopped in the middle of the path. I checked for snakes, of course, then looked at Max. "Max, I could never get bored with you. I'm sorry if I've made you feel like that was even possible."

"All I know is that I want to see things through your eyes. I want you to know that even though on the surface I live a boring routine, I want to be part of your magical world."

"Magical world?" I laughed. "I don't think it's magical." I paused and looked into his eyes. I was standing in the middle of paradise, with the man of my dreams, whose focus was to impress me. "Okay, maybe it is a little magical." I smiled as I held his gaze. "But only because you're in it."

"Kindness will get you everywhere." He grinned. We shared a quick kiss. "But I mean it, Sammy. I want to be part of all this with you."

I fell silent. My instincts were to bring up the topic of our working together again, but I didn't want to ruin the moment by bringing any tension into it. Max knew what I wanted—for him to quit his job and take a chance with me. He clearly wasn't interested. I didn't want to pressure him when he had gone to all of this trouble to make our honeymoon special.

"I love you, Max. You'll always be part of everything I do. Don't ever doubt that."

"You know that's part of the reason I planned this

hike. I mean, we could be in Vegas, or on a cruise ship with all kinds of activities, but I really just wanted to spend time with you. We've been so busy—what with the wedding and your books—that the best luxury to me was to get some uninterrupted time with you."

"And then I started formatting my book." I cringed. "I'm sorry about that."

"No need to be. I know it's important. But out here, all that matters is us and nature, right?"

"Right." I nodded and slid my hand into his.

When we reached the first checkpoint, I was surprised to see that there was a picnic blanket spread out with an assortment of dishes and drinks waiting for us.

"Wow, what a set-up!"

"I figured we'd be hungry by now." He waited for me to sit down and then sat down beside me. "There's fresh fruit, muffins, water, coffee."

"Max, this is amazing. I didn't even know something like this was possible." I hesitated a moment and then met his eyes. "It must have cost a fortune to do all of this."

Max was silent for a few moments as he set out some plates.

"Max?"

"Hm?"

I shifted on the picnic blanket. "Are you sure that we can afford all of this?"

Max met my eyes. Then poured some water into a

cup for me. He spoke in a calm tone. "Do you think I would have planned it if we couldn't afford it?"

"I didn't mean it that way. I just mean—well, you went to all of this trouble, but I don't need all of this."

"You deserve all of this and more, Sammy. Don't worry about the money."

I tried to enjoy my muffin. I really did. But my mind kept turning back to the numbers. Sure, Max made a good amount of money at his job, but he also had bills—and the wedding had been expensive too.

"It's just that I'd like to contribute."

"Sammy." Max set his cup down on the blanket. "I don't want to talk about finances."

"Alright, okay." I took another bite of my muffin. I looked at the beauty around me. I tried to focus on anything else. But my mind kept adding up the costs. The three days in a honeymoon suite, all of the activities, a helicopter ride, a catered hike—and from the sound of it, Max had a lot more planned. How could he afford so much? How could *we* afford so much?

"It's just that, it kind of affects both of us now. I mean, doesn't it?" I met his eyes.

His lashes tightened and his lips twitched. He blew a heavy breath through his lips.

"Really, Sammy? We can't just enjoy this?"

"I'm not allowed to ask about our finances? We're married now. Your debt is my debt."

"Sammy!" Max's eyes widened. "Are you kidding me?

Do you really think I'd do something that would jeopardize our future?"

"No, of course I don't think that. But I don't think it's out of line for me to ask. I mean, we are merging our lives here, Max; don't you think I should know about it?"

CHAPTER 7

Max rested his weight on his hands and leaned back as he looked at me.

"Sammy, can we drop this, please?"

"You're not going to answer me?"

"Not now I'm not. Not while we're in the middle of our honeymoon, that we're supposed to be enjoying. I'm not going to list every dime I have and what I did or didn't spend it on."

"That's not fair. I'm not asking you to do that. But you know my finances fluctuate. My books are doing well right now, but will they continue? I can't even get the formatting right! What if I mess something up?"

"So, you're worried that I might not be financially stable because your income might not be as stable as you like?" He sat back up and reached for my hand. "Sammy, I would never do anything to shake our foundation. We will always have everything that we need."

"I'm sorry."

"No, don't be sorry. Tell me the truth. Why are you worried? It's not just about the honeymoon, is it? Am I not being straightforward enough with you?"

"Max, it isn't that. As amazing as this change is, as wonderful as it is, as grateful as I am to be your wife, you have to realize that this is a huge change for me. I'm leaving the apartment I've lived in since college. I'm moving into a house—your house. I'm wondering about finances that I'm not used to not having control over—not that I want control. It's just a mess of little details that keep cropping up within me." I shook my head. "It's more about me, not you. I guess this is just a bigger transition than I anticipated."

"How could you be feeling all of this and not share it with me? Sammy, you have to know by now that you can come to me with anything. We're married now. And yes, that's a huge change—for me, too. We have to be able to talk to each other, right? Or things are going to start fraying at the edges. No hiding things."

"You're right." I nodded. "I don't know why I didn't tell you how I was feeling."

He caressed the curve of my cheek and looked into my eyes. "The important thing is that you told me now. From now on, let's try to be as honest as possible with each other. As for the honeymoon, I promise I will tell you all of the details about it, financially and otherwise, but please let it wait until after the trip, okay? I don't want any surprises to get ruined."

"Alright." I smiled. "Sure. But on one condition."

"What's that?"

"You have to feed me some of these strawberries." I laughed.

We spent quite some time sharing the delicious food. It amazed me how much better food tasted to me after a good workout, especially in the outdoor environment.

"We have to get going if we're going to make the next checkpoint on time." Max held his hand out to me. "Don't worry about all of this—someone will be by to clean it up."

"I think I could get used to this." I laughed.

The next part of our hike was a little harder. The temperature rose and Max and I focused on moving forward rather than talking. Sweat dripped down my back and gathered at the waistband of my shorts. It didn't make me feel terribly attractive.

"We're almost to another checkpoint." Max glanced over at me. "Do you have enough water?"

"Yes, I'm fine." I forced a smile.

The beauty of our surroundings offset the strain of the hike. I started to feel lightheaded from the heat.

"We're almost there." Max reached back and took my hand. "I know it's a little steep, but we can make it. We just have to keep going."

I took a deep breath and nodded. I used my free hand to wipe the sweat off my forehead before it could drip down into my eyes. My chest was so tight that it felt like it might burst. I knew that the path had turned out to be much more strenuous than Max expected. Even he seemed to be struggling a bit to get up over the ridge.

"Here we are." Max stood up straight and helped me to do the same.

Just when I was about to open my mouth to complain, I was struck by the sight before me. The ridge overlooked the vast valley below. I thought the view from the helicopter was unbelievable but the view from the ridge was even better. A flock of brightly colored birds emerged in a wave from the tree line below.

Max wrapped his arm around my waist and held me close to him. "Wow. It's better than I thought it would be."

"It's gorgeous, Max."

For a few minutes we stood in silence. I did my best to catch my breath. Then I noticed that we'd reached the end of the path. There was certainly no room for a helicopter. My heart sunk as I wondered if he expected me to walk all the way back down to where the helicopter dropped us off.

"Where do we go from here?"

"Well, for that, we're going to need a little help from a friend." Max winked at me and pulled out his cell phone.

I braced myself for whatever amazing surprise he might have in store for me.

"Hey, Marco, we're ready when you are."

"Marco?" I raised an eyebrow.

Max hung up the phone. He turned to look at me.

"Remember, this is an adventure." He held his hand out to me. "Ready to take the next leap?"

"You're making me nervous." I grinned and took his hand.

CHAPTER 8

Max led me through some thick trees and brush. On the other side of it was more of the ridge, along with a zipline. A man stood not far off from the zipline. He turned as we approached.

"Are you two ready to go?" Marco smiled.

A zipline? I peered past the ridge. The depths of the valley stared up at me. I followed the zipline with my eyes in an attempt to see where it ended. In the distance, I could see another ridge that I guessed was where we would land—or more accurately, where I would never land.

"Max." I looked at him and shook my head firmly. "I'm not doing this."

"Sammy, it's safe. I made sure that Marco was one of the best. Right, Marco?"

"Yes. The line is checked three times a day for integrity. There are emergency brakes if there are any issues, but I've never had to use them. I have helped thousands of people do this. In fact, if you'd like, I'll do it myself first—just to prove to you that it's safe."

"See?" Max smiled. "Nothing to worry about."

"That is something to worry about." I pointed to the deep valley before us.

Max nodded. He wrapped an arm around my shoulders. "Alright, alright. If you really don't want to do it, then I'm not going to make you. I'll see if I can get us a ride back down."

"Aren't you going to take the zipline?"

"Not if you're not going to." Max shook his head. "Sorry, Marco. Can you get someone up here to help us out?"

"No worries, it happens." He pulled his radio off his belt.

"Wait." I took a deep breath. "Why don't I just put on the harness and see how it feels. Maybe once it's on, I'll feel more secure."

"That's my girl." Max grinned.

"I didn't say yes. I said I'd try it out."

"Sure." Max gestured to Marco, who nodded.

Marco carefully fitted us both with the harnesses. It was lighter than I expected it to be and rather snug. The material seemed very strong.

"So how does the latch work?" I looked from the cable to the hook. "How do you make sure it doesn't wiggle around or get stuck?"

"I'll show you." Marco hooked the latch up to the cable. "See, this mechanism here will not release until it's unlocked by me or Ron, who is on the other side of the zipline. Both the cable and the latch have been tested to withstand ten thousand pounds of weight."

"And it rolls smoothly?" I walked backward a few steps to see how the movement was on the cable.

"Miss, wait!" Marco reached for me.

I didn't understand why until my heel slipped off the edge of the ridge. In the next moment there was no ground beneath my feet.

"Max!" I shrieked.

"Sammy! Hit the brakes on it, hit the brakes on it!" I could hear Max shouting at Marco.

As I whizzed over the valley my screams echoed back at me. When I managed to get my eyes to open, I did see the beauty around me. My screams faded off as I realized that I was not falling. In fact, the sensation of the wind whipping across my skin and the weightlessness that the harness provided almost had me convinced that I could fly.

I spread my arms and soared. It was such a light and airy sensation that I didn't want it to end. My body felt free from all of the constraints of society—of my expectations and the expectations of others. It was great, until I saw the ridge that approached.

I started to kick my feet. I had no idea how I would stop, or if I would land correctly. The closer I got to the ridge, the more I panicked. I closed my eyes tight. Just when I thought I would crash, I landed in the arms of a muscular man. He held me so tight that I thought I might burst. Considering that I'd nearly lost the contents of my bladder when I stepped off the edge of the upper ridge, that was a very real possibility.

"Miss, are you alright?" He breathed the question in my ear as he settled me to my feet. "Marco told me what happened. If he had used the brakes, you'd have been stuck over the valley until we could get a helicopter out to you. I'm so sorry. That must have been very frightening for you."

I smoothed the hair back from my face and took a deep breath. "To be honest, it was awesome. I mean, I was terrified at first, but once I realized I wasn't going to crash, the entire experience was phenomenal."

I had just gotten my balance when I heard Max's voice from a distance.

"Sammy, I'm coming!"

Max's shout carried through the valley as he zipped toward the edge of the cliff. I tried not to laugh as I took a step back to give him room to land. Max's arms and legs were flailing through the air as if he was trying to make the zipline go faster. When he landed in Ron's arms he looked right at me.

"Are you okay? Did you get hurt? Are you going to divorce me?"

I burst out laughing at the look in his eyes. "No, silly, I'm not going to divorce you."

"Are you sure?" Max stumbled out of his harness. "I tried to catch you but you stepped right off the edge of the ridge!"

"I know, how crazy was that? I didn't know it was so close. But I have to say, if I hadn't been so clumsy, I never would have had the most amazing experience of my life. I mean, other than marrying you, of course."

Max's eyes widened. "You liked it?"

"Sure. It's gorgeous and fun, and I can't believe I didn't want to try it."

"Wow. I think I missed everything because I was so worried about you."

"Well, then maybe we should go again." I laughed.

"Uh no, I think once was enough for today." Max hugged me so tight that I think he was afraid I might step off the ridge again with no harness. "Let's get to our campground for the night. We have a flight in the morning."

"The helicopter again?"

"Not this time." Max nodded to the guy who was helping us with our harnesses. "Thanks, buddy, it was great."

"My pleasure." He nodded to us both.

CHAPTER 9

As Max and I walked down the path, neither of us seemed very steady on our feet. Sailing through the air across a valley could make a person a little dizzy. We leaned on each other as we made our way toward a clearing. I expected to find a tiny droopy tent—or maybe a run-down cabin at best. Instead, I saw what had to be the mansion of all tents—if it could even be called a tent.

"What is this?" I looked around the large circular structure.

"It's called a yurt." Max nodded. "I looked it up."

I had to laugh at the pride in his voice. Max had certainly gone to quite some lengths to make our experience as adventurous and inventive as possible.

"I think that if we try, we might just enjoy this." I grinned at Max.

"We'd better." He tugged me toward the entrance.

The interior was as surprising as the exterior. It had a full living room, a large bed, and even a small kitchen and dining room. It was as luxurious as any hotel room, but somehow cozier and still integrated with nature.

"I tried to make sure we had some nice places to rest in between our adventures." Max patted the edge of the bed. "And after this last one, I'm really looking forward to getting my arms around you."

I sat down on the bed beside him and smiled as he wrapped his arms around me. "Max, I never thought I would enjoy that zipline, but I really did."

"See, I can still surprise you." He kissed the side of my neck. "Are you hungry? I can get something for us."

"Not now. Now I just want to lie down with you. If that's okay?"

"I thought you'd never ask." He sighed and collapsed back against the bed. "I'm exhausted."

I grinned and crawled up beside him.

It wasn't long before we were both asleep in each other's arms.

It was just about dark when I woke up. I looked for Max but the bed beside me was empty. I sat up and blinked in the dim light of the yurt.

"Max?"

There was no answer. My heart skipped a beat. I was being paranoid, but I didn't like the fact that he didn't answer me. I stood up and walked into the kitchen. Max wasn't there either. I rubbed my arms and tried to stay calm.

We were in the middle of nowhere. What could possibly go wrong?

I heard a strange snapping sound. It drew me out of

the yurt and around the side of it. Instead of a wild animal, I came across Max snapping twigs.

He looked up and smiled at me. "I thought you might be getting up soon."

"Are you building a fire? I didn't know that you could do that."

"I was in the Boy Scouts." Max grinned.

"You were? I didn't know that either."

"It's just about ready. Want to sit?" He gestured to a blanket spread out beside the fire.

"Oh yes." I plopped down on the blanket. "Do you need any help?"

"I think I've got it."

He started the fire and stoked up the flames. Then he sat down beside me. I snuggled up to him.

We had just settled in to roast some marshmallows when there was a loud growl from the nearby trees.

"What's that?" I leaned in closer to Max. My marshmallow fell off my stick and into the flames.

"I'm sure it's just the wind. It's easy to imagine things out here in the wild."

I nodded. Then the growl came again. "Max, I'm not imagining that."

"No, you're not." He sighed. "Stay here. I'll check it out."

"What? Why? We should just go inside."

"No way. We have more marshmallows to roast." He stood up and walked toward the trees. I watched him go.

Then all at once headlines started to flash through my mind.

Groom Abducted by Wild Beasts on Honeymoon, Blushing Bride Too Good to Save Her Groom.

I jumped to my feet. How could I let him go in there alone?

I crept to the edge of the trees. "Max?"

All I heard was the creak of the tree branches. There was no other sound. I stepped a little further into the trees. New headlines flashed through my mind.

Bride and Groom Devoured on Their Honeymoon, Hungry Bear Has a Big Meal.

"Sammy, I told you to stay there." Max's voice made me jump.

"I couldn't let you go out here by yourself."

"My hero." He laughed and hugged me. "Don't worry, whatever it was, is gone."

"Maybe we should give up on the marshmallows and head inside."

"Sounds good." Max doused the fire, then we headed back inside.

We snuggled up on the bed again. I traced a fingertip along the curve of his cheek and down the side of his neck.

"Mm, that's nice." He turned into my touch.

I met his eyes. "Max, this has been amazing."

"There's more." He kissed me.

"You're all I need."

"You have me. But first thing in the morning, we fly to our next destination."

"Another one?" I shook my head. "What could be better?"

"I think you'll enjoy it." He pulled me close. "We need to make the most of this time."

His words brought me right back down to reality.

The honeymoon was fantastic, but it would come to an end. Then there would be real life to deal with—my books, Max's work, settling into a new home. All of that felt like so much to handle. All I really wanted was to stay wrapped up in Max's arms.

"Sammy, can I ask you a question?"

"Hm?"

"What exactly were you planning to do if you encountered a beast ripping me to shreds?"

"Oh please, that wild animal would have nothing on me. It would be in pieces before it would have the chance to break your pretty skin."

"Pretty skin?" He raised an eyebrow. "That's a little creepy."

"That your skin is pretty or that I would defend it so viciously?"

"Uh, both?" He laughed. "I love my creepy Sammy."

"I love my pretty-skinned Max."

CHAPTER 10

Early the next morning Max woke me up. "We have to hurry or we'll miss our flight."

I still felt groggy from the odd sleep pattern of the night before. "Okay, I'm moving." I yawned.

"Sammy, really." He gave my shoulder a light shake.

"I'll be right there." I burrowed my head into the pillow. The next thing I knew, the blanket was gone and Max had his hands around my ankles. With one hard tug I slid down to the bottom of the bed.

"Max!"

"We can't miss this flight."

"Alright, alright." I forced myself to get up.

Within minutes we were on the path again. "Do we have to hike far?"

"No, not far. It's only beyond that bend." He pointed ahead of us. "Sorry for the rush this morning."

"It's okay. Part of the adventure, right?"

"I guess I didn't time everything just right."

"Max, you worry too much. This is fantastic—it's all perfect. Let's hurry." I grabbed his hand and began to run up the path.

Max managed to keep up with me. We rounded the bend and ran right onto an airstrip. The smallest plane I'd ever seen appeared to be waiting for us.

"Oh no." I looked over at Max. "You're really going to make me get on that thing?"

"I could always ask for the helicopter instead." He grinned.

"That's it. Next honeymoon I'm making the travel arrangements."

We walked toward the plane.

"Next honeymoon?" He looked over at me.

"Sure, we have to do another one every ten years. Isn't that a rule?"

"If it isn't, it should be." He opened the door to the small plane. "Get in. Paradise awaits us."

I took one last look at the wilds that surrounded me. It struck me that were it not for Max, I never would have seen this place.

As soon as I was settled in the plane I rested my head against Max's shoulder. Despite all the beauty that I'd witnessed over the past few days, paradise for me was still tucked in the crook of Max's arm.

We flew over the wide-open sea. It was an amazing sight, but it was more than just sparkling calm blue. It was expansive, and it left me humbled. It was easy to see myself as small as a grain of sand, when the world was stretched out so wide beneath me. All of the troubles that weighed my mind seemed minuscule when compared to the vastness of the ocean.

I wound my hand around Max's and looked into his eyes. "I love you, Max."

"I love you too, Sammy. I can't believe our honeymoon is almost over, though." He frowned. "I have to say I'm a little sad to see it end."

"Me too." I squeezed his hand. "But we have a lot to look forward to."

"I promise not to leave my socks lying around."

"What?" I laughed.

"I mean, this is going to be the first time we live together. I just don't want you to get annoyed with me and my single man habits."

"You do realize I have a few single woman habits too, right?"

"Like what? Dancing around with nothing on?" His eyes widened as if he might be hopeful.

"Uh, well, maybe every now and then." I grinned. "Let's see...there's eating crackers in bed. Plus, I never ever hang the towel right in the bathroom."

"Oh, that's horrible." Max shook his head. "I don't think I can live with that. The crackers in bed are one thing, but the towel hung wrong? Seriously?"

I laughed. "I guess we'll both have things to adjust to."

"I'm looking forward to adjusting with you." Max pointed out the window toward a large island. "That's where we're landing."

I stared at the sand. I blinked a few times and then rubbed my eyes. The way the sun reflected off it gave it a strange tint. A minute later I couldn't see the sand anymore.

The plane taxied down the runway and ground to a rather abrupt stop.

"You okay?" Max looked over at me with a half smile.

"Yup, just fine."

"Are you sure?"

"Yes, I'm fine."

"Then would you mind taking your fingernails out of my skin?" His smile broadened.

I looked down at his hand and realized that I'd dug my nails into it during the landing.

"I'm sorry!" I released his hand with a few red semicircles left behind.

"It's okay, that was a pretty bumpy landing. But it's the last one, I promise. Our next flight will be on a nice big smooth airplane."

"Ugh, I don't want to talk about the flight home just yet."

Max helped me out of the plane. We thanked the pilot, then walked across the tarmac to a waiting cab.

"I had all of our things from the first hotel shipped to this one, so everything we need will be there."

"You think of everything, Max."

"I try." He rubbed the curve of my knee. "I'm glad you're having a good time."

"A good time? No. The greatest time of my life? Yes." I grinned.

As we drove through a small town, it was easy to see that it was set up for tourists. There were brightly colored shops and a large selection of restaurants. But in between the flashy buildings, I could see little patches of the true island life.

There were small cottages with chicken-wire fences. Some had goats roaming through the yards along with chickens. I smiled to myself as I saw a few little boys, shirtless and shoeless, that chased each other around. I loved getting this visual of what life was really like on the island. Although I had been enjoying the luxury of the beach-side hotels, real travel to me meant seeing different ways of life—not just different versions of the same hotel room.

CHAPTER 11

The cab pulled into a small parking lot. In front of us was a white modular building.

"Here you are."

"This is it?" Max eyed the driver. "Are you sure?"

"This is what you see." The driver held up a brochure that showed a towering hotel. "This is what you get." He gestured to the small building.

"No, this isn't right. This can't be right. Sammy, I swear this is not what I reserved."

"Max, don't worry about it, I'm sure we can make do. Let's just check it out."

Max frowned. He jerked open the door of the cab. "Wait here, let me see what's going on." Max stormed up to the small building.

I gave him a minute and then followed after him. I waved to the driver to let him know it was safe to leave.

When I opened the door, Max turned to look at me. "I asked you to wait in the—" He stared out the window at the cab as it drove off. "Sammy?"

"Don't worry, Max, whatever it is, we can work it

out." I smiled at the sleepy man behind the counter, who said:

"We're the only place on the island with vacancies."

"Well, I guess we're staying here then."

"Number three." The man slid a key across the counter to us.

"What about the gazebo?" Max frowned at the man.

"Don't worry, it's all set." He winked back at Max.

"Alright, let's check it out."

"Don't let it get to you, Max, I'm sure it's better than you expect."

Max slipped his hand into mine. "Please tell me that you have a good feeling about this."

"I have a feeling that we can make it good."

"I hope you're right."

We rounded the corner of the white building and saw six smaller buildings.

"This was not what was in the brochure, not at all." Max groaned.

"Don't worry about the brochure. This is where we are right now. Let's make the best of it."

"Well, since we no longer have a cab—"

"Max." I squeezed his hand. "Positive thoughts, my love, positive thoughts."

"I positively think this is not what was in the brochure."

We walked up to the bungalow that matched our key.

"See, it's not so bad, is it?"

"Well, it's no yurt, but it will have to do." He unlocked the door and swung it open.

I started to step inside, but he swept his arms around me before I could.

"Max! Put me down!"

"No way, I'm going to do this every chance I get."

Max didn't put me down until he reached the bed. The bungalow was a studio with a bathroom and a small kitchen. The bed was small but cozy.

"Oh, this is nice. I think you need to test it out." I tugged hard on his hand and pulled him down on the bed beside me.

"Oh, this is nice, you're right." Max nestled his head against my stomach. "Cozy and warm."

"Stop it." I laughed.

"What? You said to test it out." He grinned and kissed the curve of my neck. "We have the place for two days, how about we don't leave this bed?"

"Hm. As tempting as that sounds, I'm pretty sure that lovely sound and scent drifting through the window is the beach calling my name."

"Oh, fine." He sighed. "If we must leave, I suppose I'll allow it—on the condition that you skinny-dip with me."

"Nope, not doing that."

"What? Sammy, remember—adventure?"

"Adventure does not include getting sand in unmentionable places, trust me."

69

"Okay." He laughed. Then he sat up in the bed. "Wait a minute, are you speaking from experience?"

"Never mind, Max. I'll get changed." I hopped up out of the bed and rushed for my suitcase and the bathroom.

"Wait a minute, I want to know how you got sand in unmentionable places." Max tried to follow me but I closed the bathroom door before he could catch up.

"One day I might just tell you, Max…one day."

The warmth of the sun danced across my skin, but it was nothing compared to the warmth of Max's touch. As we left the bungalow behind, he glanced over at me.

"Okay, you were right, this is better than I expected."

"How can it not be when we're together?"

"Good point."

We stepped off the wooden walkway and onto the sand that lined the shore.

"Max, look at the sand!" I tightened my grasp on his hand.

"It's amazing, isn't it?" He kicked his toes through the sand, which was a color that I'd never seen before—it had almost a pinkish hue to it.

"Wow." I shook my head. "Another thing that I can say is a total surprise."

"How about wine under the stars?" Max gestured to a small gazebo on the beach. "It's ours for a few hours."

"Wonderful."

CHAPTER 12

As Max led me into the gazebo my heart lurched. I didn't intend for it to. It just happened. The magic of the water, the sand, the clear blue sky, and the warmth of his skin against mine was enough to make me feel like the luckiest woman on earth. Except, I didn't want it to end. I wanted it to continue—and to expand.

"Max, wouldn't it be great if we could explore new places together?"

Max sat down beside me in the gazebo and opened the bottle of wine that waited for us in a chilled bucket. "Sure it would."

"Our life could be so free. We could travel anywhere we want and explore as much as we want. What could be better than that?"

Max was quiet. He poured us both a glass of wine, then handed one to me.

"Is that something that you would like, Max?" I took the glass and tried to meet his eyes.

"Who wouldn't?" Max chuckled.

"I'm serious, Max. We have our lives ahead of us, and we can choose how we're going to live them. Right now, we can decide what our future will be like."

"Sammy, not everything can be planned." He took a sip of his wine.

I watched as he settled his gaze to the water, instead of on me.

"Maybe not, but this can be. If it's something that we really want, we can make it happen. But maybe it's not what you want? You can tell me the truth, Max."

"Well, like you said, this is the beginning. Our lives are opening up before us. There's a lot we need to sort out. But right now, this is about celebrating the present—this moment. We'll be headed back home soon, and we can deal with all of that when we do."

"But, Max—"

"Please, Sammy…" Max leaned forward and met my eyes. "You told me to relax about the hotel not being a hotel, and I did. So can you relax about this?" He reached out and took my hand. "The sun is setting, we have wine and we're together. Isn't that enough for just this second?"

"Yes, it is." I sighed and took another drink of my wine. "Why don't we take a walk?"

"Good idea."

My muscles were tight with tension as we walked. I didn't deal well with not knowing what would happen next. I had to bite into my bottom lip to keep from asking again and again, until I got a clear answer. The further we walked, the more I began to relax. The sunset eased the remainder of my tension with its colorful display. I focused on being in the moment with Max.

When he spun me into his arms to kiss me, I was ready to let go of all control and savor the moments we shared—until I felt a pinch.

"Ouch!"

"Hm? Teeth?" Max leaned back. "Sorry, I was swept up in the moment."

"No, it wasn't you. Ouch!" I hopped up on one foot.

"Sammy, what's wrong?"

I looked down at the sand. A vicious-looking crab was poised to strike my ankle again.

"Ah!" I pulled away from Max. "It's out to get me!"

"Just stay still. It will move past you."

"No way! That thing's after me!" I turned and started to run away from the crab. The crab scuttled right after me.

"Sammy, stay still!" Max chased after us both.

I splashed into the water. I thought maybe the crab wouldn't chase after me. I was wrong. It splashed right into the water. Max followed after.

"Get away, beast!" I kicked my feet in the water to scare the crab off. Max plucked me right up out of the water.

"Don't worry, he'll end up on our plate one day."

I laughed and slung my arms around his neck. I knew

in that moment that even if Max decided not to quit his job, our life would be just as adventurous and wonderful.

Early the next morning I plopped down hard on the bed next to Max. He muttered in his sleep. I tickled the tip of his nose with my fingertip.

"Mm, stop." He swung his hand in the air and sighed.

"Max, guess what!"

Max rolled over in the bed and opened one eye to look at me. "No."

"What do you mean no?"

"You asked me to guess what, and I said no." He yawned.

"I know that, but why not?"

"Because I want to sleep. Preferably, I want to sleep curled around your beautiful naked body. So why are you out of bed and dressed?" He sighed.

"As tempting as that sounds, I just spotted something amazing on the beach."

"Really?" He opened both eyes. "What?"

"You're not even going to guess?"

"Alright, fine. There's an army of crabs waiting to attack you?"

"There's a yoga class." I smiled. "If we hurry, we can catch it."

"Yoga is not really my thing." He nestled back down in the blankets. "Let me know how it goes."

"Max!" I put my hands on my hips, partially because I knew that I looked great in my yoga pants. "I want you up and out of that bed."

"Why?" He moaned and buried his face in his pillow.

"I got in a helicopter for you, Max, remember?" I poked his big toe, which stuck out from under the edge of the blanket. "The least you can do is crawl out of bed and spend some time on the beach."

"But—but I've never done yoga." He sat up. With the heel of his palm he dug into his eye. "I'm tired, Sammy."

"Nope. Sorry, Max, you're not getting out of this one. Once you start doing it, you're going to love it. Just think, if you were home with me, we could do yoga together every day."

"Thrilling." He forced himself out of bed with a grunt. "Alright, alright—just give me a minute."

"Don't take too long, I don't want to miss saluting the sun."

"Saluting the sun?" Max groaned again. "Does that mean no sunglasses?"

"Max!"

"Okay, okay!" He hopped over to the bathroom.

I tried not to grin. Even when Max and I argued, I found him impossibly adorable.

CHAPTER 13

When Max emerged from the bathroom he looked a little more awake.

"Let's go." He slung an arm around my shoulders. "But I'm not going to call anyone guru."

"Why would you call anyone guru? You watch too much television."

"I watch too much television? Don't think I don't know about those late night TV binges. Who's your TV boyfriend right now?" He raised an eyebrow.

"Only you, baby, only you." I did my best not to blush.

"Uh-huh—me and that detective that runs around in a kilt."

"Well, yes, him too." I smiled.

"I'll be right out. Don't worry, no kilts in here."

I laughed as he closed the door. I loved that Max and I could still banter the way we did when we were just best friends. A part of me had been afraid that when we got married I'd disappear into the "wife" role and lose that position of best friend. So far that hadn't been the case.

The group on the beach had everything set up when Max and I arrived. It was clear that this was not their first routine together.

"Good morning." I smiled at the yoga instructor.

"Good morning. Welcome. Please take any mat you like and find a space that resonates with you."

Max arched an eyebrow in my direction. I pointed to the pile of mats. "What color would you like?"

"Uh, yellow, I guess."

I grabbed him a mat and chose my own.

As we walked to an open area on the sand, I couldn't tear my eyes away from it. The pink shade fascinated me. "I didn't know sand could be this color."

"It's beautiful, isn't it?" Max situated his mat next to mine.

"Oh, you might want to leave a little more space. I have a bad habit of losing my balance when I do yoga."

"Alright." Max slid his mat over.

"Now, Max, just take it easy. A lot of these people aren't beginners, so they may do more difficult positions or hold the pose for longer. It's not a competition."

He smiled. "You say that like I might feel the need to compete. I'm sure it can't be that hard."

I looked at him for a moment. I was well aware that Max could be very competitive. "Just remember what I said and don't push yourself too hard."

"I hear you, I hear you." Max nodded.

The instructor began to go through the first movement.

I knew the movement well, so I watched Max to see if he would need any help.

His brows seemed to knit with confusion. He tried to position his foot correctly, but he had it in the wrong spot.

"Just move it over here." I pointed to the right spot on his mat.

"I know, I'm just stretching." Max grunted his words.

I eased into position, then glanced over at Max. He was about halfway into the movement. I could see that his right leg was trembling with the strain of the position.

"Just relax, Max. Only stretch as far as what's comfortable."

"It's okay, I'm fine." Max gritted his teeth.

I tried to focus on the teacher. We changed positions.

Max ended up with his back to a group of about six women.

"Now, raise your arms—slowly, slowly. Now bend them back over your head—slowly, slowly."

"Is that even physically possible?" Max sounded out of breath. Beads of sweat lined his forehead.

"Are you okay?"

Before Max could answer, he started to sway.

I tried to move in time to catch him, but my own muscles burned from the stretch, as I was a little out of practice. Before I could reach him, he fell backwards, right into the group of women behind him.

One by one, they all tumbled—like dominoes—until there was one big pile of yoga students on the mats.

"I'm so sorry!" Max jumped up. He turned to offer his hand to the women he'd knocked over.

I tried not to laugh. For once it wasn't my clumsiness that had interrupted the class. I held back my amusement and helped the others back to their feet as well.

"Sammy, I can't do this. I'm sorry." Max shook his head.

"Max, everyone has mishaps when they start out. I know I did. Don't let it stop you." I took his hand and guided him back onto the yoga mat. "Just get centered. Stay in the moment, right?"

"Right." He sighed and wiped the sweat from his forehead.

"Alright, everyone, let's move through some breathing exercises." The instructor looked right at Max. "Sometimes focusing on breath can bring everything else in our body into alignment."

Max frowned and glanced over at me.

I tried not to smile. It wasn't that I took pleasure in Max's embarrassment; I was just relieved that for once it wasn't me. I reached out and took his hand in mine. When he met my eyes, I smiled.

"You're doing great."

He shook his head. "I don't think there's anything

great about what I've done."

"It's the effort and the experience that counts, Max. Try to breathe. It will help you to relax. This is how you get naked—without taking your clothes off."

"Wouldn't taking my clothes off be a lot easier?" He sighed.

The instructor shushed him.

I tried not to giggle while I focused on my breath. I drew it slowly in and out. I recognized that I'd lost that sense of living in the moment. I wanted to structure what came next, instead of accepting it. I released my desire to control and felt my body ease deeper into a state of relaxation.

"Wonderful, everyone, wonderful. Now open your eyes and look out at that wide-open ocean. Allow your heart and mind to be just as wide and open. There truly are no limits."

CHAPTER 14

As the class broke apart Max looked over at me with a quirked brow.

"You do this all the time?"

"Not as much as I should." I handed the mats back to the instructor. "This was a good reminder that I need to get back into the routine."

"Wow, Sammy. I have to admit I didn't know how hard this was. I thought it was just a bunch of twisting and breathing. I'm worn out."

"I'm glad you did it with me."

We started to walk back toward the bungalow.

"Excuse me, excuse me!"

I turned to find a woman walking up behind us. She was about the size I was when I first started my journey, with bright green eyes and thick red hair. I couldn't help but notice how pretty she was.

"Yes?" I smiled.

"I'm sorry, I don't mean to disturb you." She looked past me at Max. "I just wondered if I could talk to you for a moment."

"Max, I'll catch up with you, alright?"

"Sure." Max nodded and jogged up the beach.

Once we were alone, I turned back to the woman.

"I'm Samantha."

"Oh, I know who you are." Her cheeks grew dark with blushing.

"You do?" I raised an eyebrow. "Have we met before?" I was feeling slightly confused because I really couldn't place the women's face.

"Not exactly. This is going to make me seem like a stalker…my name is Jenny, and I've been following your blog for a long time." Her eyes widened. "I've bought your books and I recognized you from your picture. I couldn't believe it at first—that it was really you."

"Jenny, you're one of my readers?" My smile spread wide. "Wow, what a coincidence that we would both end up on the same beach in the same yoga class."

"I know, it's crazy. I wasn't going to say anything, but I thought maybe there was a reason we were both here. You know?"

"Oh, sure. Maybe we were meant to meet each other."

"Maybe." She lowered her eyes.

"Is something wrong?"

"It's just that I've been following your blog for a long time. I admire you more than I could ever say. But I can't seem to get my head together the way that you did. You seem so confident and comfortable in your body. But, it was terrifying for me to come out on the beach just in this." She gestured to her yoga pants and t-shirt.

There was nothing about the outfit that exposed her, and yet I knew exactly what she meant. There'd been many times that I'd felt naked despite being fully clothed, just because I tried something new—something that I hadn't thought I could do.

"Jenny, trust me, it took me a long time to get my head together too, and to be honest, I didn't do it alone. I did it with the support of some very good friends."

"I guess maybe that's the problem—I don't have a lot of support."

"You know, I didn't think I had much when I started either. But sometimes if you ask for it, you can find it. Taking classes is a great way to start because the teachers and other students are usually very supportive."

"You're right. I haven't tried that yet. Thanks so much for the advice. I can't tell you how many times I've read your blog and wished that we could just have a cup of coffee and chat."

"That's a good idea." I smiled. I needed some ideas to get the latest book of my B.I.G. Girls Club moving, and I thought Jenny would be the perfect subject. "Why don't we get some coffee?"

"Really? It wouldn't be a bother?" Her eyes widened.

"Not at all. I'll meet you at the little cafe on the corner in twenty minutes, alright?"

"Great, I'll see you then."

As I walked away my heart felt as open and wide as the sea, just like the instructor had mentioned. It was invigorating to reconnect with the entire reason I'd decided to pursue writing. I really could reach more people than I'd ever imagined.

When I caught up with Max in the bungalow, he already had the shower running.

"I'd ask you to join me but I don't think I'm even going to fit in this thing." He scowled at the narrow shallow stall. The showerhead released water in a sprinkle. "Do you want to get in first?"

"That's okay, I'll take one in a little while."

"That class really wore me out. That, and I wasn't ready to wake up." He yawned.

"Why don't you take a nap? I'm meeting someone for coffee anyway."

"What do you mean you're meeting someone for coffee?" He laughed. "Who do you know here?"

"Remember that woman from this morning? Her name's Jenny. She follows my blog. I'm just going to have a quick cup of coffee with her and give her a pep talk." I smiled.

It meant a lot to me that I could reach out to someone who was in the same situation that I'd once been in.

CHAPTER 15

"Wait a minute. Is this a honeymoon or a work trip?"
Max shook his head. "I know how important your work
is, but we don't have a lot of time left. If I'm going to take
a nap, I want to take it with you, or at least know that
you're nearby. Is that strange?"

"No, it's not strange." I smiled at him. "It's sweet,
and I agree with you. I want to spend all of my time with
you too. But this will only be twenty minutes tops."

"You know I don't even think it's really about the
coffee." He sighed. "To be honest, I feel like work has
crept into this trip. First it was the formatting of your
book, and now you're doing personal consultations." He
frowned. "I just wanted this to be time for us."

"I understand that, Max. It's really hard for me to
turn work off, because it's more like a lifestyle for me
than a job. Do you know what I mean?"

"I guess I don't. I go to work and come home. I don't
know what it's like to have my profession be a part of my
every moment."

"Is it such a bad thing?" I cringed. "I mean, it's only part of every aspect of my life because it's my passion."

He laughed a little. "It's hard to get passionate about computer tech, trust me. Although some of the people I work with are; I don't know why. I guess it does worry me a little bit—that you never seem to be able to turn it off. I don't want you to get burnt out."

"What do you mean I never turn it off?"

"You're always looking for a new chapter to write, or a new experience to share. Which is great—don't get me wrong—but if you're always thinking and looking, are you ever really experiencing? All of the things that we've shared so far—were you really there for them or were you just stuck inside your head plotting out the next few chapters of your book?" He lifted an eyebrow. "You say that you love your work, and I believe you, but there has to be room for our relationship in there somewhere too. I don't want to worry about whether the way I tickled the curve of your neck is going to end up in some blog post, or that my opinion on a meal at a restaurant is going to be on someone's bookshelf. I mean, we can't even have our honeymoon without it being invaded."

"Invaded?" I stared at him with wide eyes. "Max, I had no idea that you felt that way. I just thought that you supported what I do."

"I'm sorry. Invaded wasn't the right word. It came out wrong. Sammy, I do support your work. I do." He sighed. "Of course I do. But does it have to be all you do?

Does it have to be a part of every moment of our lives? I guess I'm trying to figure out where I fit into all of this."

I tried to hear what he was saying. I tried not to react emotionally and to allow myself time to understand his words. But the hurt that spread through my chest was too intense. I'd married Max thinking that he might want to quit his job and work with me on my books. I thought that he was as passionate about my work as I was.

"You're all of it. Don't you see that, Max?" I met his eyes. "If I've let you feel left out, I'm sorry. But you're part of every aspect of my day too. It's hard to explain, but just like I'll never be able to turn off how I feel for you, I could never turn off the work that I do."

"I guess over time I'll understand it more. I just don't want us to lose sight of our marriage. I know it's just started, but I want to make sure that we take care of it— of each other. I don't want to wake up in five years and wonder how we drifted so far apart."

"Oh Max, that will never happen." I wrapped my arms around him and held him close against me.

How lucky was I that the man I married was so focused on making sure that our marriage was as healthy and happy as it could be? But it also revealed to me that he had some insecurities of his own.

"I promise, I'll never let my work come between us. In fact, it's what brought us together in the first place, remember? I mean, if I hadn't explored myself and grown as a person I'd still be holed up in my apartment fantasizing—" I gulped back my words. "I mean—longing for you."

"No, wait a minute, tell me about this fantasizing again?" He tightened his arms around me. "Just how long did that go on for?"

"Wouldn't you like to know?" I winked at him. "But my point is, that's why I'm so passionate about this. Jenny isn't just a fan. She's a woman who, just like me, hasn't figured out how to live her life to her fullest. I think the scariest thing to me is knowing how close I came to letting all of this—us, the love we share, my career, our future together—just pass me by. All because I didn't believe in myself enough."

"I know." He rubbed one hand across the curve of my cheek. "I know you're right, Sammy. Of course you should go meet with her."

"Really? You're not going to be mad?"

"We're blending our lives. There are going to be some things I don't like and some things you don't like, but it's not up to me to make decisions for you. If that's what you feel you need to do, then that's what you need to do." He looked back at me. "And if you happen to feel that it's important to be honest with your husband about past fantasies, then you know, I'm open to hearing about them." He winked at me.

I laughed and shook my head. "You're amazing, Max."

"Better than the fantasy, or about the same?" He

raised an eyebrow. "Because there's always room for improvement."

"Max!" I swatted his arm with a playful touch.

"I'm getting in the shower before the hot water runs out. Enjoy your coffee." He smiled at me and then disappeared into the tiny shower stall.

CHAPTER 16

I thought about staying. I knew that Max wanted me to, even if he claimed to understand. But that would set the wrong standard. I had my priorities, and they didn't always match up with Max's. No matter how in love we were, we still had to retain our own personalities and desires. I'd seen too many women and men disappear into a relationship and regret it later.

As I stepped out of the bungalow, I wondered if Max would ever really want to work with me. I sensed that he had concerns about it. The way he avoided talking about it punctuated those concerns.

I walked through the streets between the large buildings to get to the cafe. I noticed an assortment of people gathered in one yard. There was a delicious scent of something cooking. The air was littered with laughter and squeals of children. Some of these people had shoes, some didn't. Some had tattered clothes, some had newer clothes. No one cared. The yard they had gathered in was overgrown—not perfectly manicured. The house was small and in need of paint. But no one paid attention to that. They were simply happy to be where they were.

That was the attitude that I wanted. I wanted to be able to enjoy whatever moment I was in, without thought of insecurity, or comparing myself or my successes with other people. I hoped that with my career I could accomplish that sense of trust.

When I arrived at the cafe Jenny was already there waiting for me. She waved me over to the tiny table where she sat.

"Samantha, I'm so glad you came."

"Me too." I smiled at her. I made an effort to push all thoughts of Max and our spat out of my mind. I wanted to be in that particular moment.

We placed our order for coffee, then my attention returned to Jenny. "How are you enjoying your vacation?"

"I'm enjoying it. It was a surprise from my sister. I think she hoped I'd meet somebody here. No so such luck."

"It'll happen." I smiled. "I never thought it would happen for me, but it did."

"Are you sure this wasn't too much trouble?" Jenny frowned. "I know it was very forward of me to just walk up to you."

"It's no trouble at all. I'm glad that we can talk. I feel like I never get to know the people that are reading my blog. I mean, I read comments here and there, but to meet someone face to face is really great."

"I'm glad you feel that way, because to be honest I

could really use all of the help that I can get." She shook her head. "I'm to the point that I don't want any mirrors in my house."

"Aw, Jenny, that's no way to treat yourself."

"I know. But I just can't seem to get past this anger I feel inside. Like, I let this happen, I let myself gain this much, and now I have to face the consequences."

I sat back in my chair and toyed with the handle of my coffee cup. "I think one of the most important things I did early on in my journey was to learn to love my body as it was—for what it was. I try hard to do the same now."

"It's easy for you to do now, though—you look great."

"No, I still look in the mirror and see a million flaws. That is the actual problem—not the weight or the flaws, but what we see in the mirror. I mean, if I wanted to, I could tear my appearance to shreds. The difference is, I learned not to want to. I got more out of loving myself than abusing myself." I met her eyes across the table. "There's only one person who will ever love your body the way you do. No one else gets to love it, or live in it, just you."

"I never really thought of it that way." She nodded. "All of this time I've been acting like my body is the enemy."

"That's so hurtful. How can you ever expect to grow and blossom if that's what you're nourishing your mind and heart with? Thoughts like that will only halt your progress. Don't get me wrong, I've felt the same way in the past, but it was a hurdle that I had to overcome to reach my optimum health."

"You're right." She sighed. "I guess I get caught up in the spiral of these negative thoughts and self-hatred. Then to make myself feel better, I binge."

"And some people starve themselves, some people use exercise as a punishment—it's all part of the same pattern of thought that tells us that there's something wrong with us, something wrong with our body— something that we've done wrong. The truth is, our body is all we have. It's our vessel, it's our tool. Without it, we can't exist. The more we tear it down, the less functional it becomes. People get so focused on the right diet, the right exercise, the right amount of calories, but they skip over the most important part. Do you love your body? Do you love you?"

"Wow." She smiled. "This is just what I needed to hear today, Samantha. You have no idea how much you've helped me."

"You helped you by being brave enough to step out of your comfort zone and approach me. You could have decided to walk the other way, but you valued yourself enough to honor your desire to connect with me. I know how nerve-wracking taking that first step can be. If I hadn't moved outside of my comfort zone over and over again, I wouldn't be on my honeymoon right now with the love of my life. The choices you make matter."

"I'm so glad that you chose to spend this time with me. I know it took away from your time with your husband, and I can't tell you enough how grateful I am to you. I feel so inspired to really make a change in my life. I don't want to hide from who I am anymore. I want to learn to love myself."

"It's one little step at a time." I reached across the table and squeezed her hand. "We've had years of being programmed to believe that we need to be something more than who we are. It takes time to recognize that we have everything we've ever needed right inside of us."

"Thanks, Samantha." She stood up from the table.

I stood up as well and opened my arms to her. As we hugged, tears formed at the corners of my eyes. No, this wasn't work for me. Max was right. It was an essential part of who I was, and it seeped into all aspects of my life because of that. I wouldn't have it any other way.

"Good luck, Jenny. Keep me up-to-date on your journey, okay?"

"I will, I promise."

CHAPTER 17

As I watched Jenny walk away, I felt as if she represented the me I was a few years ago—shy, uncertain, and terrified of being seen. So much had changed since then, and yet I would never forget what it was like to loathe my own body.

The weight of a hand on my shoulder startled me out of my thoughts. I turned to find Max behind me.

"Max, I'm sorry. I know that I was gone longer than I thought I would be and you're probably upset—"

"No, I'm not." He gazed into my eyes. "I just listened in on that conversation. I just witnessed the impact that you had on that woman's life and her view of herself. I get it now, Sammy. I can't say I really understood it before, but I get it now. I'm sorry. I never should have asked you not to meet with her."

"You had a right to, this is our honeymoon."

"And you put the health and well-being of someone else above your own needs, Sammy. I think you have a lot to teach me too." He leaned forward and offered me a soft kiss.

I returned it with a sigh of relief. I was not only glad that he wasn't upset, but also that he truly understood why I had to meet with Jenny.

"I don't think I'll ever be able to separate my work from my life, Max. I hope that won't be a problem going forward."

"It won't be." He wrapped an arm around my waist. "I promise."

"How about that nap?" I smiled at him.

"Sounds good." He kissed my forehead. Then he whispered in my ear. "Maybe you could tell me a few bedtime stories."

"Max!" I swatted him again.

When I woke up from our nap, I was instantly pleased to find myself wrapped up in Max's arms. I hadn't yet gotten used to waking up with him. It was a delicious experience every time it happened.

Max's eyes fluttered open. He smiled at me. "Did you sleep well?"

"Yes. Did you?"

"I did, yes."

"I can't believe that we go home tomorrow. What do you want to do with the rest of our day?"

"I have one last surprise for you. Will you walk down to the beach with me?"

"Absolutely." I snuggled close to him and sighed.

"But does it have to be right now?"

"I suppose we could wait a few more minutes." He kissed my cheek, then my lips.

A contented sigh escaped me as I settled in his arms. The honeymoon could have consisted of nothing more than this and I would have been happy.

"I'm looking forward to getting back home and starting our new lives together, Max. Aren't you?"

"More than you know. I can't wait until we fill our home with our memories. Sammy, I never thought my life could be as good as it is right now. You have no idea how grateful I am to share the rest of my life with you."

"Me too. It's funny—I keep expecting to be disappointed that our honeymoon is almost over, but I can't be. I just get even more excited about the future."

"I only have one regret."

"What's that?" I looked at him with some concern. I couldn't think of anything that I regretted about our relationship.

"That it took us so long to get here."

"Oh, I don't regret that." I looked into his eyes. "Max, we may not have been lovers, but we have always been friends. I think all those years of us being best friends gave us a special connection that not everyone has."

"I never thought of it that way. You're right. I wouldn't trade a moment of our friendship, just like I wouldn't trade this moment. I guess it all worked out the way it was supposed to."

"I don't doubt it." I rubbed my hand across the back of his. "I guess we'd better get going or we might never leave this bed."

"That wouldn't be the worst thing, would it?"

"Not at all."

"But I did make plans." He grinned. "Alright, up and out of bed." He stood up and pulled me up out of bed with him.

"Let me get dressed."

"Something light, we're going to be out in the sun."

"Alright. Any other hints?"

"Not a single one."

I sighed. After so many surprises I should have been used to it, but I still had that nagging need to know what I was in for.

Once I was dressed, Max and I walked down toward the water.

"Look at that gorgeous boat." The sailboat at the end of the dock had bright golden sails that stretched high into the air. The boat itself was white with a gold stripe around it.

"That's the surprise. We're going to have lunch out on the open sea." Max smiled at me. "I thought we could enjoy our last full day in paradise alone together."

"Alone?" I looked over at the sailboat. "But I don't know how to sail. Neither do you."

"Aha, but what you don't know is that I've been

taking sailing lessons for six months—just for this day."
He met my eyes. Pride seemed to be causing his to shine
even more than normal. "You will be in fully capable
hands, my love."

"Wow, now who's been keeping secrets?" I grinned.

"It was a good secret."

"A very good secret."

"We don't head out until two. I'm going to pick up
some last-minute supplies. Why don't you enjoy the beach
for a little while?"

"I could enjoy that. Just don't be too long."

"No more than an hour."

"Great."

We shared a quick kiss.

CHAPTER 18

I walked down to the edge of the water as Max headed back into town to shop. As I waded through the warm water, peace seemed to flow into every pore of my skin. The sand that shifted beneath my feet reminded me that nothing was set in stone; the environment around me constantly fluctuated.

Max had gone to so much trouble to make sure that I had a great experience on our honeymoon. He thought of such tiny details to make everything special. I wanted to do something special, memorable, for him. Our romantic relationship entered a new dimension after our wedding, one that I wasn't entirely open about just yet. It was still a little awkward to be sensual with him.

I thought it would be nice to prepare a seductive surprise for him. The very idea caused my heart to flutter. I looked over at the sailboat. Max would be back with the last of the supplies in a little under an hour. That gave me plenty of time to create a surprise for him.

I hurried back to the bungalow and changed into the bikini that he'd bought for me.

When I returned to the sailboat I looked around for anyone that might notice my actions. The beach was empty, which I thought was a little strange. Where were the swimmers and the sunbathers? Maybe everyone was having lunch.

I stepped onto the edge of the sailboat. It rocked side-to-side beneath my weight. I caught my balance when I grabbed the low metal railings on either side of the boat. Once the boat was steady, I stepped all the way onto it. The boat continued to sway. When I turned to sit down, it lurched and tipped. I drew a breath and tried to swallow back my fear.

"It's fine, you're not going to fall out, and even if you do, you know how to swim." I eased myself down into a sitting position. Then I began to slather my skin with the scented lotion that had been a bridal shower gift. It was edible.

I giggled at the thought. I wasn't sure why anyone would want to eat lotion off someone, but it combined my two favorite things—food and Max—so I figured it was worth a try.

A sharp wind caught the sail of the boat. The whip of the material made me jump. Maybe that was why no one was on the beach. The sky darkened. Maybe it would be better to wait for Max on the dock.

I grabbed the lotion and turned back to step off the boat and onto the dock. However, when I lifted my foot to step on the wooden slat, I found that there was nothing but sea beneath me. I gulped and tipped backward into the boat.

There was another sharp breeze and the boat lurched. I tried to grab the railing to keep from losing my balance but my hands were slick with the lotion I'd applied. I fell flat on my bottom in the middle of the boat.

"Ouch!" The boat rocked and lurched to one side. Only then did I realize that something had gone terribly wrong.

I was floating out to sea! I looked toward the shore, which was already quite a distance away. Could I swim for it? The sky rumbled. My heart pounded. What would the storm do to the current? I didn't think it would be wise to risk swimming.

"Max!" I screamed toward the shore, even though I knew he was likely still shopping for the last of the supplies. The louder I screamed, the louder the wind roared and the waves crashed.

The weather turned fast. It grew so dark that I could barely see the shoreline. Storms weren't unusual in tropical climates, but I had a hard time not taking it personally.

As the boat got further and further from the shore, panic began to set in. My heart raced so fast that I started to get dizzy.

I stood up and waved my arms back and forth through the air. That only succeeded in rocking the boat so much that I nearly fell over the side. I sank down to my knees in the middle of the boat and drew a deep breath.

"Be in the moment, Sammy. Be in the moment." Then I looked at the shore as it got further and further away. "No! I don't like this moment! I don't want to be in this moment! Max!" I yelled as loud as I could.

There was no one else on the water. I did spot a silvery blur under the water, but I had no idea if it was a dolphin or a shark. What I did know was that I would very likely fall out of the boat and be eaten by either a shark or a dolphin. Tears made my eyes burn. My throat tightened. It was the day before the end of my honeymoon, and I was lost at sea—in a very revealing bikini.

Would Max even know what happened to me? Would he ever find out the truth? Would he think that I left him?

As I wallowed in these thoughts my hands balled into fists. It wasn't fair. Everything had been perfect—and yet all because I wanted to be seductive, I was going to be fish food? No.

"No!" I stood up on the boat. I realized that this was quite a mistake when the boat almost tipped over. I held on tight to the railing but my hands still slid with the lubrication of the lotion. "This is not how my honeymoon ends, it is not how my marriage ends, I am not going to float out to sea."

CHAPTER 19

I looked at the sails. I knew that there was a way to move them and position them so that I could steer the boat. I didn't know how to make that happen, though. I grabbed the edge of one of the sails and tugged as hard as I could. The sail swung wildly and almost knocked me off the boat.

I flattened my body against the boat. The wind rushed over the top of me again. The boat spun in the water and then rose up on a high wave. I closed my eyes against the rain that began to fall.

As I clung to the boat I gave in to the idea that I was stuck. I could fight it and end up in the water, or I could ride out the storm with the hope that I wouldn't get thrown off the boat.

As thunder crashed through the sky, I thought about all of the steps it had taken to get me to that exact place at that exact moment. All the determination to check off the items on my bucket list had given me the confidence to start a relationship with Max. That relationship with Max had launched our engagement and marriage. All of it had led to this moment, on the rough sea, clinging to a sailboat that didn't even belong to me.

The storm began to settle. When I opened my eyes, I saw the wide-open water. When I looked in the direction that I thought shore should be, all I saw was more open water. In fact, that was all I saw in every direction around the boat. I shuddered despite the heat. I was alone with no hope of rescue. Even if I could figure out how to work the sails, there wasn't a trace of wind that remained after the storm.

The choppy water settled again to a smooth glassy state. I had nothing to block out the sun's hot rays. My body was mostly exposed because of the bikini I was wearing. Sunburn was in my near future, as was dehydration. I looked at the tube of edible lotion.

"At least I have food." I frowned. I took a lick from my fingertip. "Ugh, it's horrible. Who would even enjoy this?"

As the time ticked by, I lost track of it completely. I didn't have my cell phone or my purse. I had no idea how long I'd been on the water. The only thing I knew for sure was that I hadn't gotten any closer to land. Yet again, one of my silly ideas had ended up leading me straight into disaster.

What was Max doing? What was he thinking? He had to be worried sick about me. As terrible as it was to be out on the water, he had to be enduring much worse as he tried to piece together what had happened.

Maybe that was it. Maybe I finally had too much happiness and the universe decided to balance it out. What other explanation could there be?

The boat continued to drift. Exhausted and beyond terrified, my mind began to make up fantasies. I imagined what it would be like to be rescued by pirates—a big black boat decorated with skulls and filled with dirty sweaty men.

"Oh, Max. I'm sorry." I closed my eyes, the heat scrambling my thoughts.

Was it possible that all of the steps I'd taken to have faith in the way life unfurled been pointless? It couldn't end this way. I wiped sweat from my forehead and tried to focus in the direction I thought the shore would be.

Max had to know I was missing by now. He probably saw that the sailboat was gone too. Hopefully he had put two and two together. It couldn't take long for him to summon help. But how long would I be waiting for it?

I did my best to stand up in the boat. The sun was low in the sky. There was maybe an hour or two of light left. I tried not to think about what might happen to me in the dark. What if another storm kicked up?

"Don't panic. Panic doesn't solve anything." I sighed. "I need solutions, not problems."

I couldn't see anything on the shore, but from the flow of the water I could guess which direction it was. I dug my hands into the water to see if I could get the boat to move. My awkward paddling didn't do anything but spin the boat in a very slow circle. My arms ached by the time I gave up on the idea.

I looked at the sails again. The storm had battered them to the point that I wasn't sure they would catch any wind, but at least they were still up in the air. As long as there was sunlight, there was a chance that the boat would be spotted on the water. It was clear to me that everyone had fled the beach and the water when the storm approached. But it was calm again. That meant a rescue boat was very likely on its way.

"But will it get here before the pirates?" I laughed at myself. "Pirates—really, Sammy?" I sighed and peered down through the clear water.

The water was quite deep. I thought about swimming in the direction of the shore, but there were so many wild creatures under the water. After my run-in with the crab, and the near-death experience of Dolly the dolphin, I just couldn't bring myself to jump in. Besides that, I knew my best bet was to stay put. There were probably search planes getting closer every minute.

But what if there weren't? What if Max didn't put two and two together that I'd gone out on the boat? What if they just assumed the boat had been swept away in the storm? Max might have thought I'd met up with Jenny, or taken cover from the storm somewhere safe. Was anyone even looking for me?

I closed my eyes and focused on my breath. In and

out I breathed. The salty sea air that had once been so intoxicating to me now was a bitter reminder that I was lost at sea. I wasn't sure that I was ever going to get home again.

Another deep breath, and a slow release. Focus, Sammy. Solutions, solutions, solutions.

I focused with such determination that I slipped into a mild trance.

When I heard a loud squawk, I nearly wet my pants.

CHAPTER 20

I opened my eyes to see a seagull perched on the boat next to me.

"Oh, hello!" I smiled at the seagull. "This is a good sign. I can't be too far from shore, right? I'm so glad that you're here. You can be my friend." I tried not to think about the fact that I was having a conversation with a bird and possibly going a bit crazy.

The seagull squawked at me again. "Seagull, can you show me where the shore is?" The bird tilted its head to the side as it looked at me. Maybe it was the heat, or maybe I had lost my mind, but I began to see the seagull as my hero.

"Maybe I could tie a message to your foot. Would you take a message to Max for me? You could do that, couldn't you?" I looked around for anything that I could write a message on. I didn't have anything that I could write with, either. Then I spotted the tube of lotion. It was greasy enough to leave a mark. I tore off a piece of the battered sail and went to work. Once I had my message written, I looked at the seagull.

"Come here, little guy. You're going to save me." I reached out to grab the bird's leg, but it squawked and flew up into the air the moment I reached for it. "Wait, come back! You're my only hope!"

The seagull circled around above the boat. My stomach twisted as I realized how silly the entire idea had been to begin with. The bird wasn't going to save me. No one was going to save me.

Hot tears slipped down my cheeks. My skin burned from being in the sun for so long. My head spun from both the heat and hunger. I looked at the tube of lotion and frowned. I guessed that it was better than nothing.

When I picked it up and squeezed some out on to my finger, the bird swooped straight at me.

"Hey, watch it!" I swung my hand in the bird's direction. Then I noticed there were more seagulls circling above the boat—a lot more. "Shoo!" I waved my hands at the birds.

The birds all swooped down and landed on the boat. They surrounded me. Only then did I realize my awful mistake. The birds weren't there to help me. They were there because they wanted to eat the lotion. The lotion that was smeared all over the railings and all over my skin.

"Get back!" I stood up and waved the piece of sail at them. The boat rocked and lurched. My feet slid across the hard plastic from all of the lotion I'd coated them with. I grabbed for the railing as I lost my balance. My hand slid right off the curve of it and I tumbled head first into the water beside the sailboat.

The water splashed against my sunburned skin. It was actually a cool relief compared to the heat of the sun. But only for a moment. As I swam to the surface, I thought about how many sharks might be circling underneath me. With every kick of my feet I expected sharp teeth to clamp down.

I grabbed the side of the boat and tried to pull myself up onto it. My hands were too slippery from the water and the lotion for me to get a good grip.

"No, no, no!" I wailed. Just when I thought that things couldn't get worse, they had. I'd suddenly becoming shark bait.

The birds all flocked onto the boat and began to devour the lotion that was left behind.

"Oh, Max, we had a good run." I rested my head against the side of the boat. "I guess this really is how it will end." I closed my eyes and stopped trying to think of ways to save myself. I surrendered to the fact that I was stuck in the water, and I waited for what would come next. I had no control.

As my mind drifted in the same pattern as the waves I heard a voice.

"Ahoy there!"

"Pirates. The pirates are here. The pirates are here." Somewhere in the back of my mind I was aware that there was no need to sing. But I couldn't stop myself from singing about the pirates.

I opened my eyes and saw a small powerboat headed straight for me. At first I thought it was just my imagination, but the sound of the motor stirred me from my dazed state.

"Max?" I peered into the last of the sunlight.

When the boat pulled closer I could see two men in uniform on the boat.

"Samantha?" One of the men called out. "Just hang on, we're going to get you out of there. Don't panic."

"Okay, I'll be right here." I smiled. "But watch out for the pirates. They're on their way."

"There aren't any pirates, Samantha. It's okay. You're safe now."

"I'm here, Sammy, I'm right here." Max leaned off the side of the boat.

"Wait, we'll get a ring to her."

Max ignored the man in uniform and jumped right into the water beside me. When I felt his arms wrap around me, everything disappeared—the water, the sailboat, even the impending pirates. All I knew was the warmth and comfort of Max's arms.

"You found me. You found me, Max."

"It's alright, we're going to get you out of here, Sammy. You're going to be okay." He lifted me up to the arms of the man in the boat.

CHAPTER 21

As I sprawled out on the bottom of the powerboat I became aware that this was not a fantasy. I was safe. Max was pulled up onto the boat after me. He fell on his knees next to me.

"Sammy? Are you okay? Are you hurt?"

The other man in uniform leaned over me and pressed his fingers against my wrist. He studied me closely.

"She looks good—just needs some water." He tipped a bottle of water to my lips.

Max took it out of his hands and held it steady for me.

I still couldn't believe I'd been saved.

Max pulled the bottle of water away from my lips and sighed. "I was so worried, Sammy. What happened?"

"Uh—well, I—I don't think I want to talk about it right now." I glanced at the other two men.

I could feel the boat being turned around and the power of the motor as it sped back toward shore.

"You're lucky that thing held up in the storm," one of the men said over his shoulder. "It pushed you so far out we almost didn't find you."

My eyes widened. "Seriously? You mean I might have been out there all night?"

"Or more." The man nodded. "We were about to turn back, when we saw all of those birds."

"Birds?"

"The seagulls. It's unusual to see a large amount gathered in the middle of the water, so we thought we should check it out."

"Those birds liked you for some reason." The other man chuckled.

"Might have had something to do with this." The first man held up the tube of edible lotion.

"What's that?" Max raised an eyebrow.

"Oh, it's—uh—sunscreen."

"I don't think it did the job." Max frowned.

"Huh, I've never heard of edible sunscreen." The man holding the tube read the label. "A delicious way to enjoy a sensual massage with your lover."

"Hey!" Max's eyes widened. "Sammy?" He looked over at me.

"I was going to surprise you." I hung my head. "I thought I'd wait for you on the boat. But when I stepped on, the boat started drifting. It wasn't tied."

"The owner probably untied it because of the storm. He probably went to get a larger boat to tow it away."

"Wow." Max shook his head. "I'm sorry, Sammy."

"You're sorry? Why? I'm the one that did something so silly."

"Because I never should have left you there alone."

"Oh Max, I don't need a babysitter." I laughed. The two men in uniform both looked at me with faint smirks. "Okay, I don't normally. I just wanted to do something special for you. You've made this trip so memorable, and I wanted you to have a good memory to take home with you."

"Sammy, you didn't have to do that. It was a lovely thought."

I sighed. "Maybe, but now I just want to go home."

"First you need to go to the hospital."

"The hospital?" I shook my head. "I'm fine, really, I don't need to go."

"We'd just like to take you in—to have a look, make sure that everything's in order." The man tried to keep a straight face. "We want to ensure that lotion didn't have any chemical reaction on your skin from being in the sun so long."

If my face was already red it must have burned crimson in reaction to the man's words.

I looked over at Max and grimaced. "I'm sorry. I've ruined the last night of our honeymoon."

"You haven't ruined anything. I'm just glad that you're okay." He kissed the back of my hand. Then he stuck the tip of his tongue out and took a taste. "Mm, that's not bad."

"It's terrible. I tasted it." I laughed.

"Well, maybe it's your skin that tastes so good then." He grinned at me.

Despite the horror I had just endured, Max made me feel wonderful.

When the boat pulled up to the dock, a cheer went up from the beach.

"Are they cheering for me?" I sat up in the boat and looked at the shore.

"We formed a search party. They're just happy that you're safe."

I ducked back behind Max. "Max, I can't let all those people see me. I'm in my bikini and the color of a sunburned lobster."

"Don't you mean just a lobster?"

"No, I'm redder than a lobster!"

"Sammy, they just want to see that you're okay. You don't have to show them, but you're going to have to get off the boat somehow."

All of the people on the beach were cheering for me. Not because I had done anything worth cheering for, but because I had returned alive. They offered their support without having any idea who I was. I couldn't even stand up because of a bikini and some sunburn?

I stood up and stepped off of the boat onto the dock. The cheers grew louder.

"Thank you!" I waved to the people that were

gathered. "I'm fine now, thanks a lot."

Max touched the small of my back. His touch was gentle.

"You might be red, but you're still beautiful, love. Let's get you to the ambulance."

"Ambulance? Is that really necessary?"

"Oh, trust me, you don't even want to think about sitting on the vinyl seat of a cab." Max shuddered.

"Good point. I'll take the crisp cool sheet of a gurney."

"Don't worry, I'm going to stay right by your side."

As the ambulance drove away I held onto Max's hand. The last thing I wanted was to let him go.

CHAPTER 22

When we arrived at the hospital, Max walked beside the gurney. He didn't let go of my hand.

When I was wheeled into a room, Max remained right by my side.

Once I was settled in the room he sat down on the bed beside me. "How are you doing?" He met my eyes. "It had to be so scary out there alone."

"It was." I nodded. "I honestly didn't think I was ever going to get back to shore."

"Sammy, I wish I had been there with you."

"But the birds—"

"Sammy." He laughed. "I would have braved the birds for you."

"I would never ask you to do such a thing." I giggled. "Thank you, Max."

"For what?"

"For making the worst day of my life one of the best."

"As long as we're together we can make any day the best."

"Aw, Max, I still wish our honeymoon wasn't ending like this."

"There's still time left, sweetie. The important thing is that we make sure you're healthy."

It was such a loving moment that I hoped it would never end. Then the nurse walked in.

"Who is the patient here?"

"Sorry, I was just keeping her company."

"Is that so? I wasn't aware that being in the hospital was a team experience."

Max stared at her for a moment. "She's fine, she's just here for observation."

"So, now you're the doctor?" The nurse put her hands on her hips. "I decide why she's here, not you. Of course, if you would kindly move out of the way I might be able to examine my patient."

The nurse's abrupt nature had Max flustered, but I bit into my bottom lip to keep from laughing.

Max stood up and glanced over at me.

"I'll just be over here." Max walked toward the edge of the hospital room.

"Over here." The nurse edged him right toward the door.

"Now wait a minute. There's no reason that I can't be in the room with her. She wants me to stay, don't you, Sammy?"

I looked from the nurse to Max. "It's okay, Max. Let her do the exam. We'll be able to get out of here faster."

"Yes, Max. Listen to Nurse Diana. Out with you. And if you try to come back in here before I call you, I will find a reason to give you a shot."

"A shot?" Max's face grew pale. "You can't be serious."

"I am quite serious, young man. Now out."

I had to cover my mouth to keep from laughing.

"I'll be right outside, Sammy." Max stepped out the door.

Nurse Diana pushed the door shut behind him. "Finally, we're alone." She smiled at me.

When she walked toward me I felt a slight flutter of fear. She had been so harsh with Max, how would she react to the ridiculous reason I was in the hospital in the first place?

"So it seems we have some major sunburn to deal with. Also, you were a little dehydrated but your vitals are stable. I think that you're going to be just fine."

"Oh, good, so I can go?"

"Not just yet. I have something for you."

"It's not a shot, is it?" I cringed. "I mean, of course it's fine if it is." I resolved to be brave.

"No, it's not a shot." She laughed. "The paramedics let me know what happened on the boat. I checked the composition of the cream that you used, and I didn't see anything that should cause a reaction. Now this cream should help with the burn." The nurse handed me a tube of cream. "Don't eat this one though, okay?"

"Very funny." I sighed and took the cream. "I can't believe I did something so ridiculous."

"Oh, don't worry about that. You're young and in love, and you were just trying to do something fun. No shame in that, sweetheart. If you let other people tell you how to live your life, you'll never have a life to live." She patted the back of my hand. "You're going to be just fine. Do make sure that you use that cream though or you'll be peeling in a few days and—well, honey—no amount of lotion or lingerie is going to make that sexy."

I burst into laughter at her words and the visual that she gave me. "Alright, I promise I will use the cream."

As the nurse left the room I was reminded of the surrender I'd felt in the water. She was right, I could relax. Yes, what happened left me embarrassed and sunburned, but it was over. I was still alive and lucky enough to get another shot at an amazing life.

A light knock on the door drew my attention.

"Come in."

Max poked his head into the room. "Is it alright if I come in? Is the nurse still here? Is she coming back? Did you see her?"

"She's gone." I grinned at him. "You're safe."

"Good. She was a bit cranky, huh?"

"She's okay—just doing her job." I smiled. "I can understand that."

"Well, your only job right now is to get better."

I nodded and sat up in the bed, but I couldn't look

right at him. My chest ached with regret. It was our last night, and I would spend it trying not to move.

"Sammy? What's wrong?"

"I'm sorry, Max. I just feel like I've taken away our last chance to enjoy our honeymoon."

"Sammy, today I thought I lost you. Just having you here with me is a miracle. How could that be disappointing? Besides, our honeymoon doesn't end just because we go back home, does it?" He smiled. "I mean, it doesn't have to. Being in a beautiful place is great, but any place is beautiful when I'm with you."

"That's it, you win."

"Win what?"

"Best husband ever!"

"Remember that in a year when you find my underwear under the bed and whiskers in the sink."

"I'll try." I laughed.

As we left the hospital there was no question in my mind that I'd still be grateful for Max in a year—and in fifty years.

CHAPTER 23

Max got me settled at the bungalow.

"I'm going to go get us some dinner, will you be okay while I'm gone?" He met my eyes.

"I'll be fine. I promise—no wandering off onto boats."

"Okay, good." He smiled. "I'll be back soon."

After Max left I found it hard to get comfortable. The sunburn was not as painful as I'd expected, but my body was stiff and sore. I decided to call my best friend Stephanie to get my mind off of things. Her phone only rang twice before she picked up.

"So she is alive!"

"Huh?"

"Girl, I thought you'd at least call me when you got to Bermuda."

"I'm so sorry, I didn't even think about it. Max has kept me busy."

"I bet." Stephanie chuckled.

"That's not what I meant!" I laughed.

"Sure, sure."

"How are things back in the real world?"

"No way, I'm not talking about me. I want to know what you've been up to! Oh my god, I've been dying for some details. How is everything going? Did you like the honeymoon surprise?"

"I sure did. Max did a wonderful job. I feel closer to him now than I ever have before."

"That's great. I can't say that I'm not looking forward to you coming home. I miss you."

"I'll be home soon, trust me. I think I've had enough adventure for a while."

"Uh oh, did something happen?"

"All that matters is that I was not eaten by a shark. Let's leave it at that."

"That's funny. Wait, are you serious?"

"Yes, I am. I think I've also developed a phobia of dolphins."

"But dolphins aren't scary."

"They are now." I laughed. "And pirates too. No more pirate movies for me."

"Okay, you're going to have to tell me this story."

"I will, but not just yet." I sighed and settled back against the bed. "I'll see you soon, Stephanie. I can't wait to get settled in and get things straightened out with my next book release. I've got so much to do when I get back."

"Don't worry, I'm sure that Max will help you. That's the plan, right? For you two to work together?"

"Well, I'd hoped. But it doesn't seem like it's going to work out that way. That's okay. I'd rather Max do what he's passionate about, instead of being forced into something that he doesn't want to do."

"Why don't you just talk to him about it? Max is reasonable."

"I think I've mentioned it enough times. I'm just going to let it go. If it's something that Max really wants, then he'll come to me about it."

"I can't see how working together with you would be anything but perfect for you both, but okay. Don't worry, we'll figure it out when you get back. You still have a few hours of honeymoon left, so get off the phone and go enjoy it."

"I will, Stephanie. Thanks for everything!"

When I hung up the phone I felt the slightest bit of sadness. I didn't want to dwell on it. I thought of ways to distract myself.

I decided to check on my blog. I only had a little bit of time before Max would be back, and there wasn't much more that I could do. It would give me an opportunity to anticipate the amount of work I had to do when I got back—plus I wanted to see if Jenny had updated me.

When I logged into my e-mail I found a note from an address I didn't know. I opened it up and discovered that it was a message from a promoter that wanted to offer me the opportunity to do a book tour throughout France. It never even occurred to me that someone might offer me such an amazing opportunity.

I read over the details, realizing that the offer appeared to be legitimate. The woman who extended it owned several small bookstores throughout France and she wanted to give new authors an opportunity to showcase unique work. Apparently my work was unique enough for her.

My chest swelled with pride. It was an honor to have such an offer extended to me. However, when I noted the dates of the tour my heart sank. It was only a month away. That meant I'd need to spend the next few weeks preparing and planning, with very little time to get settled into my new life with Max.

How would he feel about my work taking me away from him so soon? I frowned. In the past I never would have hesitated to seize such an amazing opportunity, but I had to think for two now. Max had made it clear to me that our marriage was his priority. Was it mine too?

I shook my head and closed the computer. I hoped to be able to push my concerns out of my mind, but they resurfaced the moment I thought of going home. Could I really turn down what might be my big break? Could I really expect Max to understand that I had to take off on a tour that could last weeks, just after we were married?

CHAPTER 24

"Dinner!" Max walked in with a few bags of food. "I hope you're hungry. I may have overdone it."

"I'm starving." I sat up and scooted to the edge of the bed.

"Were you working?" He nodded toward the computer.

There it was—the chance to tell him about the e-mail, to ask him what he thought and talk it out. The curve of his lips and the flush of his cheeks made him look so happy. I didn't want to do anything to further damage the remainder of our honeymoon.

"Just checking on a few things. Oh, and I talked to Stephanie."

"How is she?"

"She's good—looking forward to us coming home."

Max spread the food out on the small dining room table. "I'm looking forward to it too. I can't wait to see your personal touches throughout the house and get to snuggle with you on the couch as late as we want."

"Really?" I joined him at the table. "Is there anything you're nervous about?"

"No." He looked at me. "You?"

"Maybe." I laughed. "I've never lived with anyone before."

"I'm not just anyone." He smiled. "I'm the best husband ever, remember?"

"Oh, yes." I grinned.

"Seriously though, as long as we communicate and we're honest with one another, I don't see what could be hard about it." Max shrugged. "We're already great at communicating and always honest with each other, so I'm not worried at all."

"Neither am I." I bit into my bottom lip. Again I thought about telling Max about France. I just couldn't bring myself to do it. Not just yet.

The first bite of food that hit my tongue tasted so good. I hadn't eaten since breakfast and I was ready to scarf down everything that was in front of me. After I shoveled in a few bites, I suddenly stopped. I recognized that my hunger was not just hunger for food, but hunger for something more. If I weren't careful I would slip back into my old habits of binging to quiet my emotions.

"Isn't it good?" Max finished off his last bite.

"Too good." I laughed. I took a few more bites, but paid attention to enjoying the flavor and the texture of the food. I ate for the purpose of nourishing my body, for the pleasure of the process, not to silence an ache or anxiety within me.

"Let me clear this up and then we can set up shop in front of the television. Okay?"

"Okay." I smiled.

Max took his time as he gathered everything off the table.

I stood up and moved to the bed. Just the sheet against my skin hurt. My body felt even stiffer. I suspected it might get worse before it got better.

"Alright, we have some DVDs, some snacks, and plenty of sunburn cream." Max settled on the bed beside me. "I think we're fully equipped."

"What movies did you get?"

"There wasn't much of a selection. I did get one that I—"

"Max!" I swatted the DVD right out of his hand. "That is not even close to being funny!"

"What?" He smiled with wide innocent eyes. "You don't want to watch *Jaws*?" He picked the DVD up from the floor and laughed. "I'm sorry, I couldn't resist."

"Hmph." I threw a pillow at him.

"Alright, how about this one—a nice romance." He held up the movie. His lips trembled and his shoulders shook as he held back his laughter.

"*Titanic*? Nice!" I couldn't help but laugh with him as he tossed the DVD down on the bed beside me.

"Alright, so maybe no movies tonight."

"Honestly, I'm exhausted. I know it's our last night,

but I could really use some sleep." I looked at him with a slight frown. "You don't mind, do you?"

"Not at all. You need to recover from today." He stretched out on the bed beside me. "I love you Sammy, sunburn and all."

"I love you too, Max. Even if you have terrible taste in movies."

I closed my eyes. I tried to sleep. My skin burned, but that wasn't what kept me awake. The decision about whether to go to France kept popping up in my mind. Without question, if I were not married I wouldn't even hesitate to go. So why was I held back?

I peeked over at Max, who'd had no trouble falling asleep. He snored and kicked his right foot.

That was why.

Because I didn't want to spend nearly a month not sleeping in the same bed as Max. I didn't want to miss out on his cute little snores and foot twitches.

I sighed and tried to force the thoughts from my mind.

CHAPTER 25

As I drifted into sleep my body relaxed. I awoke to a strange cry. It wasn't exactly a scream, and it certainly wasn't an animal. I forced my eyes to open all the way. It was dark. Oddly, the bed seemed to be rocking. I blinked and wondered if the dizziness might be one of the symptoms of sun poisoning.

"Max?" My voice sounded strange to my own ears. The bed lurched from side to side. My heart fluttered with fear. For an instant I thought I was back in the water. Maybe I never was rescued; maybe it had all been a hallucination. I struggled to sit up, only to find my wrists were weighed down by heavy shackles.

"What in the world?" I moved my wrists back and forth. The chains rattled as they dragged across the floor. I wasn't even in a bed. I was on a thin cushion. I sniffed the air. A thin cushion that smelled like it belonged in a trash heap. "Max? Hello?"

My mind raced. The last thing I remembered was Max's cute snore. How did I end up in some strange place shackled to the floor?

I heard the sound again above my head. Then sunlight poured down from above me. I squinted against it. Once my vision cleared, I could see that a door had been opened. A man stuck his head into the open door.

"All hands on deck!"

Only then did I realize that there were other people around me. They scrambled to their feet. They all smelled about the same as the mattress and wore clothes as dingy and tattered. My stomach lurched as I realized that wherever I was, was likely not a good place.

One of the men that moved past me paused to unlock my shackles. "That means you too."

I stumbled to my feet. All at once it struck me that I smelled just like everyone else. Ugh, what kind of shampoo would get that scent out?

"Hurry up, or you'll be walking the plank!" The man clapped a dirty hand against my back.

I stared at him with wide eyes.

"The plank?"

I made my way up the steps and out through the door. The first thing that struck me was the hot salty air.

"No!" I gasped and looked around me.

I was on a very large ship. The ship was surrounded by water that stretched as far as I could see. "No! I can't be here!" I stomped my foot.

"Settle down there and swab the deck." A man dressed as a pirate tossed me a sponge mop.

I looked at it with confusion. Since when did pirates use sponge mops?

"Get to work!" The man barked.

I looked into his eyes and was startled. It wasn't just any pirate. It was Max.

"Max, what's going on here? Is this another one of your surprises? I don't like it. Not at all."

"You don't have to like it, it's your job now. You do what I say, when I say it. Now get to work."

He turned and stomped off. I stared after him.

"This can't be real." I shook my head. "I must be hallucinating."

"Do what he says, or it'll be the sharks for ya." A short man beside me nudged me with his elbow. "Or the dolphins—they're always hungry."

"Dolphins?" I blinked. I started to push the mop across the wooden deck. None of what was happening made any sense, and yet I felt compelled to obey Max's command.

A few minutes later he returned.

"Nice job. Now, what's to eat?"

"To eat? I don't know. Fish?"

"We had fish last night. Is that all you're ever going to make—fish?"

"Max, can we go home?"

"This is your home now." He smiled at me. "Remember? I'm the best husband ever!"

I gulped back a scream. My head spun. "No, this can't

be real."

"Oh, it's real alright. Want me to show you just how real?" He grabbed me by the elbow and led me to the edge of the ship. A long wooden plank extended out into the water. The same short man nudged me with his elbow—hard enough to make me yelp.

"It's a nice plank, isn't it? One of a kind. Got it when we were in France."

"Up on the plank!" Max pointed to it.

"No, no, I won't."

"Tough girl, huh? Alright then." Max picked me up—just as he'd carried me over the threshold—and placed me on the end of the plank. I tried to turn back toward him, but the sharp tip of a sword pierced my back.

"Walk the plank! Walk the plank!" All of the voices joined together to force me toward the end of the plank. Every time I tried to turn back, I was met with the sharp poke of Max's sword.

"Let me off of here!" I began to cry. "Max, I love you!"

"I know you do. I love you too. Now get your sexy bottom in that water! Watch out for Dolly!" He gave me a hard push with the flat of his sword.

I began to fall straight toward the water. It was the same sensation I'd experienced when I fell off the side of the sailboat. Then I heard the sound again. It was the squawk of seagulls. An entire flock of seagulls. They swept under me and pulled me right up into the air.

As I soared through the air with the seagulls as my sail, I looked back over my shoulder at the pirate ship. Max smiled at me. He leaned on his sword and waved.

I woke up with a jerk. The movement made my skin burn with pain.

"Ow." I mumbled into my pillow. My pillow, which didn't smell like anything on a pirate ship.

I sighed with relief when I realized that it had all been a dream.

CHAPTER 26

I tried to go back to sleep, but the thought of Max as a pirate kept me awake. I had to admit that he'd been pretty sexy with that sword.

I sighed and sat up in bed. I did my best not to wake Max as I slid off the side. My mind filled with thoughts of the offer to tour France. Was that what the dream was about? The images were so strange that it was hard for me to figure anything out from it.

I paced back and forth through the small bungalow. One thing stuck out from the dream. I couldn't let marriage prevent me from moving forward with my career, and I knew deep down that Max wouldn't want me to do that either.

I opened up my computer and sat down in front of it. I read over the initial e-mail. It was such a wonderful offer. I knew that Stephanie would be over the moon with excitement if I told her about it. So why did it hurt so much to even think about it?

I toyed with the idea of sending an e-mail back for more details. Before I could start typing I received another e-mail. It was from the same woman. She requested a response and gave me her private cell phone number as well as an invitation to contact her at any time.

I decided to do some digging while Max slept. Maybe if I knew more about this woman and her business, I'd have a better idea of what to do next.

I spent the next few hours in research mode. I found out that the woman — Terry Donne—was a big fan of pugs, owned several bookstores throughout France—as well as belonging to a larger network of bookstores throughout the world—and had never been married, at least not that I could find any mention of.

As I dug further into her information, I saw that she'd pursued several decades of education, had traveled extensively, and met quite a few big name celebrities and politicians. Terry seemed to be living the life that I'd always longed for. It was a life of adventure, meaning, and freedom.

Was it so wrong that a big part of me wanted that too?

I noticed that there were many positive reviews about her bookstores online.

By the time I completed my search I was certain that I wanted to meet this woman, even if I didn't decide to work with her.

"Sammy?" Max blinked in the dim light of my computer screen. "What are you doing?"

"I'm sorry, I was just looking at something."

"At what?" He squinted at the time on my computer. "It's two in the morning."

"I couldn't sleep."

"I'm sorry. Do you need me to put some more cream on your back?" He started to sit up.

"No, I'm fine. I'm just going to try to go back to sleep." I closed the computer and crawled back up beside him in the bed. Nestled close to him, it didn't take very long for me to fall asleep again.

I opened my eyes to find Max staring straight at me. I jumped a little.

"Oops, I didn't mean to frighten you."

"It's okay." I blinked and sat up. "I just thought you were a pirate for a second there."

"A pirate?" He laughed. "Is that from one of those fantasies you have about me?"

"I'm still not telling you, Max!"

He groaned and flopped back against the bed. "How are you feeling?"

"Better." I ran my fingertips along the skin of my forearm. "A lot better."

"I had something planned for this morning, but I didn't know if you'd be up for it."

"What is it?"

"A champagne breakfast. But it's down in the gazebo. I just didn't know if you wanted to go out in the sun. I understand if you don't."

"I should be fine. I'll just stay covered up." I smiled and leaned over to kiss his cheek. "Let me just get dressed. I'll meet you down there if you want."

"Okay, that'll give me time to make sure everything is in place. You know this place and their false advertisement."

"I'll be down in a flash."

"Great." Max rolled out of bed and threw on some clothes.

I envied how casual he was about getting dressed. I wondered if I'd ever get to the point that I'd feel comfortable enough to just toss something on and walk out the door.

Once Max was gone, I looked for something to wear. A chose an airy dress that I hoped would not irritate my sunburn.

I was about to walk out the door to join Max when my attention was drawn to my computer. I just wanted to check to see if I'd gotten any more e-mails. It would just take a minute.

I sat down with my computer.

One of the first notes I saw was from Jenny. It detailed her new workout regiment and her own personal goal to be brave enough to go up and talk to people she was interested in meeting. I smiled at the news. I took a minute to write a quick note of support to her. Then I moved on to my other e-mails.

I hadn't received anything else about the book tour. My heart lurched as I wondered if I'd missed my chance. How long would Terry wait for a response? I decided to seize the moment and give her a call. What could it hurt just to find out some more information? I glanced at the door. Max was waiting, but I would only be a minute or two more.

CHAPTER 27

I dialed the number that she'd give me in her e-mail and waited. While the phone rang I tried to do the calculations of time zones.

"Hello?"

I was surprised by the softness of her voice. Maybe I'd expected her adventurous life to have weathered her voice; instead it was perky and bright.

"Hi, I'm sorry. I hope I'm not bothering you. This is Samantha Bradford. You sent me an e-mail about a book tour?"

"Oh, yes. Samantha, I'm so glad you called. I can't wait to speak to you. Unfortunately, I have something to attend to right this minute. Can I call you back in a few hours?"

"Sure, thanks. That'd be great."

I gave her my phone number, and just as I was hanging up the phone Max opened the door the bungalow. He looked from the phone to my computer.

"What's going on? Are you coming down?"

"Yes, I am—just got caught up in something, sorry."

"It's alright, but leave the computer here, okay? Computers and champagne don't go well together."

I smiled and closed the computer. "I couldn't agree more. Let's go enjoy that champagne."

Max carefully took my arm in his and we walked down to the beach. I still couldn't get over the pink sand. When I looked out at the water I shuddered. What had once represented peace to me now seemed vast and intimidating.

"Looking for pirates?" Max led me to the gazebo.

"You're the only pirate I'm looking for." I grinned.

As we settled in to share our champagne a light breeze carried through the gazebo. Max leaned from his deck chair toward me.

"I love this time with you. I know your work is important, but it's nice to see you without a computer in your lap."

"Oh, it's not that bad!"

"No, you're right, it isn't." He sipped his champagne. "It fascinates me that you can create such inspiring content."

"Really?" I scrunched up my nose. "I thought maybe it would bore you."

"How could it ever bore me?" He shook his head. "You forget that I've watched this entire journey, Sammy. I've even participated in some of it. I've seen you go from this shy person to this daring vivacious woman, who not only lives a wonderful life, but is generous enough to help others."

"Okay, okay, that's enough lavishing of compliments." I hid behind my champagne glass.

He reached out and took it from me.

"I mean it, Sammy. I'm proud of you and everything that you've accomplished. If I've ever made you feel differently, I'm sorry for that."

"You haven't. I guess I'm still a little insecure in some ways." I met his eyes. I felt the urge to ask him about working with me again, but I didn't want to ruin the moment with conversation that had seemed to start arguments in the past.

"I hope I can support you enough that those insecurities disappear."

"Well, it's a two-way street, you know, Max. I want you to feel as supported as I do."

"Are you kidding? Best husband ever?" He handed me back my glass. "I think it's pretty clear that we have each other's backs. I just want you to remember that you can come to me about anything."

My chest tightened as it occurred to me that this was another opportunity to reveal the offer to travel to France. The words formed in my mind. I opened my mouth to speak them, and they just didn't come.

"Thanks, Max. I love you."

"I love you too. I know that it's our last day here, but I'm actually looking forward to getting back home."

"Me too. I have so much to do." I frowned. "I have

to figure out what I'm going to do about the next book release." I rambled on for a moment, then clamped my hand over my mouth. "Oops. I'm sorry. I'm talking about work again."

"Sammy, it's okay. Try not to worry too much. I'm sure everything will work out." He raised his glass to me. "Let's toast to tomorrow, the first day of the rest of our lives."

"To tomorrow." I clinked my glass with his.

We both swallowed the remainder of our champagne. We strolled on the beach for some time as the morning gave way to midday.

"Our flight's at six, so we'll have to be in the cab by four."

"No problem." I nodded and squeezed his hand. "One flight away from being home."

"In our home." He smiled. "I love saying that. I don't think I'll ever get tired of saying that."

"I like it too." I leaned my head against his shoulder for a moment. The waves rushed up across my feet. I dug my toes into the sand. Even though I'd lived in the same apartment for so long, I had never really set down roots. This would be my first time living in an actual home.

"I can't wait to unpack."

"Well, maybe you can wait until your sunburn is better?" Max grinned and kicked a little water at me.

I jumped back away from the splash. "Hey, watch it!"

"Sammy, don't move!" Max stared with wide eyes at

the sand behind me.

"What?" I stared back at him. I didn't move a muscle.

"I think a friend of yours wants to say goodbye."

"What in the world are you talking about?" I looked over my shoulder just in time to see the crab lunge at me.

"No!" I jumped forward and right into Max's arms.

He laughed as he swung me safely away from the crab. "What's wrong? No kiss?"

"Not for the crab, but for you, always." I kissed him as the crab disappeared into the water.

I lost myself in the kiss we shared. I forgot all about the sunburn, the offer to go to France, and even the crab that seemed to have it in for me.

CHAPTER 28

When we finally untangled, Max sighed.

"I guess we have to start getting ready to go. I thought we could just get some food at the airport. What do you think? Is that alright?"

"Yes, that's fine." I tried not to feel disappointed at the mention of the airport. We had to go home sometime.

As we walked back to the bungalow I kept a close eye out for the crab.

"Max, I don't think I can ever thank you enough for all that you did to put this together. I'm sorry that I ever doubted you."

"You doubted me?" He raised an eyebrow. "I don't believe that for a second."

I laughed.

He pulled the door open for me, then paused. "You know what? I forgot something. There's one more thing that I have to do. I'll be back in just a little while. Is that alright?"

"Sure, it's fine. Anything I can help with?"

"No, it'll be quick. Just something I need to pick up."

"Alright, I'll be here."

I stepped into the bungalow and Max closed the door behind me. Alone in the bungalow, my heart was heavy. It was the last day of our honeymoon, and I wasn't sure I was ready for everything that would unfold at home. I wished that I'd told Max about the offer. He was the person I always turned to for advice, so why was I holding back?

I shook my head. I wanted so badly to plan and prepare. What about the book release? What about handling all of the tech stuff by myself? I couldn't even format my own book! The more I thought about it, the more frustrated I became. Then I remembered being in the water.

I was lost at sea, I was shark bait—with very little hope of rescue. I did everything I could to control the situation, and when that failed, I finally surrendered. I gave up on trying to control anything. I accepted what was and settled into the flow of the moment. That was when help showed up—when I stopped trying to make everything happen myself. That was when I was plucked out of the water and placed back on the path I wanted to be on.

Maybe that was the point—to give in and let things fall into place as they would. I'd made every effort to try to get Max interested in working together and traveling the world. I needed to just let it go, and let things unfold naturally. If that meant traveling to France on my own, then maybe that was exactly what I should do.

I packed up our clothes and toiletries to get it out of the way. As I slid my computer into my travel bag, my phone started to ring. I picked it up to see that it was the number that I'd called earlier that morning.

"Hello?"

"Hi, Samantha? It's Terry Donne. I'm sorry I didn't get back to you sooner."

"That's fine. I'm actually traveling this evening, so this is the best time for us to talk."

"Great. I wanted to discuss the details of the offer."

"Terry, before you go any further, I just want you to know that I'm not sure if I can accept."

"Just hear me out—that's all I'm asking."

"Of course. I'd be glad to."

"Your books are very popular here in France. As you know, women of all cultures struggle with body image and self-esteem issues. My goal is to support new authors and spread material that I think is positive and can serve a purpose. That's why it's important to me that you consider my offer. I'm willing to pay all your expenses and can assure you that you will have beautiful places to stay."

"It's a very generous offer—and it all sounds very exciting. It's just that the timing may not be the best for me."

"Oh?"

"You see, I just got married."

"Oh." She cleared her throat. "Are you not going to continue to write?"

"Yes, of course, but I don't know if it's the right time for me to be going to another country for weeks."

"I understand your concern, Samantha, but I do wonder—what kind of advice would you give to one of your readers in this situation? I find your work very bold. I doubt that you would let anything hold your characters back. Is it purely fiction for you?"

I bit into my bottom lip. Her words hit me hard. She was right. If I were writing this event as a chapter in one of my books, the character would accept the offer without hesitation. But this wasn't fiction. This was real life. This was my marriage on the line.

"It's certainly not fiction to me. It's how I've changed my life."

"I don't mean to be insulting. I'm just genuinely curious. I have other authors that I can extend the offer to. If you'd like, we could revisit this next year. But I have to say in my experience it's best to promote while a book is popular. People are fickle, and they lose interest fast. If they can put a face to a name, it really leaves a lasting impression."

"I understand." I tightened my grip on the phone. "Could you give me just a few days to think it over?"

"Sure, take a week. But Samantha, I want you to understand the scope of this project. This launch would take place in France, but it would continue on through many countries. I'm connected to a worldwide network of bookstore owners, and they are very interested in having you come also—it would essentially be a world book tour for you—and your husband, of course, if that's a feasible option for you both. I just want you to understand that if you say no, you're saying no to a chance to see the world. So take a week and think about it. Any longer than that and I'll most likely be looking at some other authors. No matter what you decide, I admire your work, Samantha, and I hope that one day we will be able to work together. Oh, and congratulations on your marriage."

"Thank you." I could barely edge the words out.

My mind spun with the information that she'd just given me. I was being offered a world tour? It was everything I'd ever dreamed of—at exactly the wrong moment. My heart wrenched at the thought of leaving Max's side. No matter how much I wanted the adventure that was offered, it wasn't something I could ever say yes to—not when it meant leaving Max behind.

CHAPTER 29

Just after I'd hung up the phone, I heard the door open to the bungalow. I swallowed hard and did my best to hide my emotions.

"Max, I packed us up."

"Oh?"

He stepped into the bungalow and looked across the room at me. "Thanks for doing that."

"Sure, no problem. We don't want to miss our flight. I have lots to do when we get back."

He smiled. "Wait, we have at least a few more minutes we can enjoy."

I nodded and walked over to him. I did my best not to look right at him. "Did you find what you needed?"

"Sammy?" Max cupped my chin with his palm and turned my face toward him. "You're upset? Is it about leaving?"

"No, it's not. Max, I'm fine."

"You're not fine." He set his jaw and locked his eyes to mine. "Let's not start hiding from each other. Not now, alright? You've been secretive about something. I know that the only reason that you would hide something from me is because you think it would upset me, or to protect me somehow. So out with it, please? I want us to start our tomorrow off right."

"Okay." I closed my eyes for a moment and then opened them again. "The truth is—a businesswoman in France has made me an offer, but I'm not going to take it."

"An offer?" Max quirked a brow.

"She wants me to do a book tour."

"Wow! That's fantastic, Sammy! Why didn't you tell me?"

"Because, Max—it's next month and we've just gotten married. I haven't even unpacked yet. It wouldn't be right for me to take off so soon."

"Wait a minute." Max laughed and shook his head. "Do you think that now that you're my wife, you've got a ball and chain? Do you think I'm going to lock you away in the basement unless I need a sandwich?"

"Max!" I rolled my eyes. "Of course I don't think that. But like you said, our marriage is important and I don't want to do anything to weaken it."

"No, no." He shook his head. When he met my eyes his gaze was stern. "Nothing will ever weaken it, Sammy. The only thing that could strain our marriage is if you compromise who you are to please me. I loved you when you were Sammy, my best friend, who tripped over everything. I loved you when you were Sammy, my girlfriend, who had a hard time learning to trust me. I love you now—more than ever—Sammy, my wife, who is going to change the world one word at a time. If I thought for even a moment that you were holding yourself back for me, I would never forgive myself. Do you understand that?"

I nodded and blinked back the tears that burned my eyes. "I understand. Max, this is such an amazing opportunity. It's a world tour, actually. I could travel to all of the places that I've dreamed of visiting. But it isn't you that's holding me back. It's me. I don't want to do any of it—not without you."

"You'd really want a husband tagging along?" He smiled.

"Only the best husband ever." I wrapped my arms around him. "Do you really think it's okay if I say yes, Max?"

"You don't need my permission, Sammy."

"I'm not asking your permission. I'm asking my best friend for some advice. Is it the right thing for me to do?"

"I think it is. In fact, I know it is. But first, before you accept the offer—before we board that plane—I need to give you something."

"Another surprise?" I wiped at my eyes.

"Last one, I promise—for a while anyway." He winked.

"What is it?" I smiled.

"This." Max held out a small wrapped present.

I looked down at the present.

"After all you've done for me, Max—you shouldn't have."

He pushed the present toward me. "Open it, please." His eyes widened with excitement.

"Alright. Thank you."

I took the present with trembling hands. I had no idea what it might be, but Max always managed to plan the best surprises.

CHAPTER 30

I unwrapped the gift as quickly as I could. Inside the wrapping was a small white box. It looked like there might be a necklace or bracelet inside. I lifted the lid of the box and found a very odd item. Max's face stared up at me from inside the box.

"What's this?" I picked up the laminated picture and looked at it. "Is this your employee badge?"

"Yes, it is." He smiled. "I thought you might like to have it."

"Okay?" I raised an eyebrow. I managed to curve my lips into a pleased smile. "Thank you."

Max laughed. "Don't worry, there's an explanation too."

"Oh, good." I laughed with relief. "What is it?"

"Sammy, the truth is—I already quit my job." His eyes sparkled. "I quit before we even got married—well, actually I was getting ready to quit and then the company let me go, which was so much better. I used some of my severance to pay for the honeymoon, that's how I was able to pay for so many of the extras."

"You what?" I stared at him. "Max, am I awake?"

"You're awake. When you mentioned us working together, I thought it would be great."

"But this whole time you've been acting like you hadn't decided." I shook my head and widened my eyes. "Why didn't you just tell me?"

"To be honest, Sammy, I thought maybe the honeymoon would be a test run to see how we worked together. Don't get me wrong, I have no doubts about our relationship, but I was afraid that adding work to that situation—well, would it put too much strain on us? Would we be able to separate our personal lives from our work lives?"

"All of this was your way of testing that out?" I frowned. "That's a lot of work to do to find out if we can work together."

Max laughed. "I know. I might have taken things a little too far. I wanted to surprise you at the end of the honeymoon. You know—a way of embarking on our new journey together. But you kept trying to get an answer out of me." He shook his head. "You were a bit relentless."

I was in such shock that I couldn't even form words. A small part of me was a little upset that he'd kept the news from me, but that part disappeared the moment I looked into his eyes.

"You really want to do this? It's not just something you're doing to please me?"

"I really want to do it, Sammy. Maybe I won't be on the front lines with you changing lives, but knowing that my support helps that goal in any way means a lot to me. I've worked at the same company for so long. Every day I go in, I do my job and I come home. But never once, in all of that time, did my efforts have the kind of impact that one shared conversation over coffee had on Jenny. That's doing something—that's contributing. I want to be part of that. No question."

"Max, that's just what I was hoping for. I can't believe that you feel this way too. Just when I thought that our lives couldn't get more perfect, you go and get more perfect."

"None of that perfect talk, Sammy, right?" He winked at me. "I couldn't imagine toiling away in some office while you're out changing the world one book, one person at time. I get it now. I get why you can't turn it off. It's who you are. That's not something you can turn off."

"Oh, Max, I'm so happy!" I wrapped my arms around him in a tight hug. "Ouch! No! That was a bad idea!" I backed off with my arms spread.

"Yes, we might have to hold off on the hugs until after that sunburn heals." Max leaned in without touching my body and kissed me on the lips. "How's that? Better?"

"Mmhm." I sighed as I looked down at my bright red skin. "Maybe the next place we travel can be a little less sunny."

"Maybe. But it'll still be paradise, as long as I'm with you."

I met his eyes and smiled. I knew then why every romance novel in the world had ever been written—because every woman had the right to hope to experience the kind of love that I had stumbled right into.

My journey was just beginning—with Max, with my world tour, with whatever came next. I treasured every single step that had led me to that moment—the good, the bad, the embarrassing, and even the sunburn.

"Let's get in contact with that woman and let her know that you accept her offer."

I pulled out my computer and we sat down together to send the e-mail.

As Max leaned over me to show me how to change the text color in my e-mail, I felt flushed—not just because of the sunburn.

I was excited.

I knew in this moment that my entire life had been leading up to this—that I was doing exactly what I was put on this earth to do. As I leaned in to give Max a quick kiss on the cheek, I couldn't believe that I'd be living out the rest of my dreams with my best friend, with my husband.

I reached under the table, gave myself a little pinch on the leg, and grinned.

It was real.

In a month, Max and I would be embarking on the

trip of a lifetime together!

A NOTE FROM THE AUTHOR

Fictional character, Samantha Bradford and the Single Wide Female books are written for every woman out there who has struggled with their weight, self-esteem and any number of issues that we all face as we work to become the best versions of ourselves that we can be.

These books are meant to be light-hearted and fun, with the hope that they will also inspire you to make your own "bucket list" of sorts—and to REALLY live your life to the fullest, loving yourself completely as you do so.

Lillianna loves to hear from her readers and can be contacted via her website where you can also download a complimentary book.

LilliannaBlake.com

ALL TITLES BY LILLIANNA BLAKE

http://Amazon.com/author/lilliannablake
*Check the author page for current list of titles

Single Wide Female in Love

#1 The Date
#2 The Girlfriend
#3 The Fiancée
#4 The Wife

Single Wide Female: The Bucket List

#1 Learn Pole Dancing
#2 Start a Blog
#3 Learn to Cook
#4 Create a Masterpiece
#5 Run a Marathon
#6 Go Skinny Dipping
#7 Start Online Dating
#8 Learn Yoga
#9 Be a Mentor
#10 Crash a Wedding
#11 Be a Movie Extra
#12 Join a Writing Group
#13 Enjoy a Spa Day
#14 Donate Blood
#15 Learn Poker
#16 Get a Tattoo

#17 Host a Dinner Party
#18 Publish a Book
#19 Walk Across Hot Coals
#20 Learn to Swim
#21 Learn to Meditate
#22 Quit My Job
#23 Learn to Salsa
#24 Fall in Love

Other Single Wide Female Titles
My Valentine's Day
St. Paddy's Day Disaster
A Bunny Tale
Sammy's Christmas List

Becoming Zara
*how the B.I.G. Girls Club came to be

B.I.G. Girls Club
The Rockstar's Girlfriend
The Former Model

Visit the author website at LilliannaBlake.com to get on the notification list for new releases and to receive a complimentary book to learn what inspired Sammy to begin her bucket list.

www.ingramcontent.com/pod-product-compliance
Lightning Source LLC
Chambersburg PA
CBHW060946180626
46817CB00004B/1731